W9-ACQ-438

"*These* green eyes are no longer safe in a pouch around my neck, eh? They will be safer in your hands."

I was startled. "Mine?"

"Who will suspect there is anything of value in the possession of a cabin boy? No one!"

I shook my head. "No, sir. I lose things!"

"Like what?"

"Didn't I almost lose my life?"

The captain playfully lifted an eyebrow. "But your life was a trifle. These are emeralds!"

"What if I run away with them!"

"Run where? You are trapped, you know. I will have to trust you."

I looked again at the gems. Those two confounded stones in my pocket were going to weigh a ton. Then I gave a shrug. "Well, if I lose them, it'll be your funeral."

"No, shipmate, it will be your funeral."

BY SID FLEISCHMAN

The Whipping Boy

The Scarebird

The Ghost in the Noonday Sun

The Midnight Horse

McBroom's Wonderful One-Acre Farm

Here Comes McBroom!

Mr. Mysterious & Company

Chancy and the Grand Rascal

The Ghost on Saturday Night

Jim Ugly

The 13th Floor

The Abracadabra Kid

Bandit's Moon

A Carnival of Animals

Bo and Mzzz Mad

Disappearing Act

The Giant Rat of Sumatra

or Pirates Galore

BY SID FLEISCHMAN

ILLUSTRATIONS BY JOHN HENDRIX

A GREENWILLOW BOOK

HarperTrophy®
An Imprint of HarperCollinsPublishers

LIBRARY
FRANKLIN PIERCE UNIVERSIT
RINDGE, NH 03461

Harper Trophy® is a registered trademark of
HarperCollins Publishers.

The Giant Rat of Sumatra or Pirates Galore
Copyright © 2005 by Sid Fleischman, Inc.

All rights reserved. Printed in the United States of America. No part of this book
may be used or reproduced in any manner whatsoever without written permission
except in the case of brief quotations embodied in critical articles and reviews.
For information address HarperCollins Children's Books, a division of
HarperCollins Publishers, 10 East 53rd Street, New York, NY 10022.
www.harperchildrens.com

The text of this book is set in Adobe Caslon.
Book design by Chad W. Beckerman.

Library of Congress Cataloging-in-Publication Data

Fleischman, Sid.
The Giant Rat of Sumatra or Pirates Galore / by Sid Fleischman.
p. cm.
"Greenwillow Books."
Summary: A cabin boy on a pirate ship finds himself in San Diego
in 1846 as war breaks out between the United States and Mexico.
ISBN-10: 0-06-074240-2 (pbk.) — ISBN-13: 978-0-06-074240-9 (pbk.)
[1. Pirates—Fiction. 2. San Diego (Calif.)—History—19th century—
Fiction. 3. California—History—1846–1850—Fiction.
4. Mexican War, 1846–1848—Fiction.] I. Title.
PZ7.F5992Gm 2005 [Fic]—dc22 2004042457

❖

09 10 11 12 13 LP/CW 10 9 8 7 6 5
First Harper Trophy edition, 2006

LIBRARY
FRANKLIN PIERCE UNIVERSITY
RINDGE, NH 03461

FOR JULIAN

Contents ☞

The

Giant Rat of Sumatra

or Pirates Galore

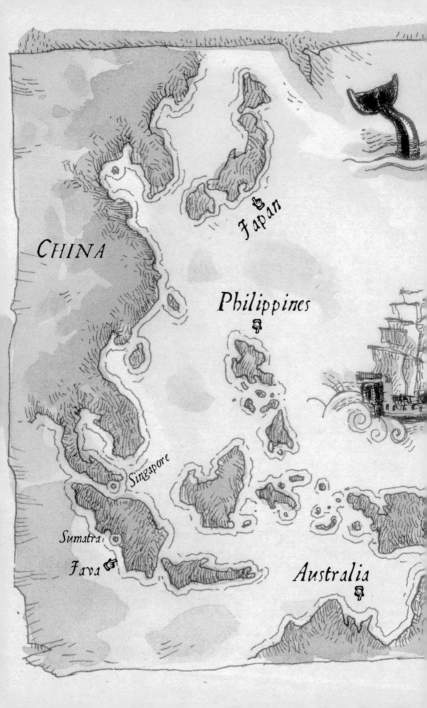

CHAPTER ● 1

The Giant Rat of Sumatra pokes its nose
off the coast of California, and
things begin to happen

My story begins on the night an owl blundered into the belfry and rang the church bells. The town awoke with a sense of doom. It was an omen. Something evil was in the air.

Through drifts of fog, an exhausted sailing

ship came creaking into the harbor. After a long voyage, it was down to its last puff of wind and its last cask of fresh water.

Under its needle nose of a bowsprit clung a dreadful figurehead—a giant rat. The creature, painted mustard yellow, had been carved out of a mahogany log felled in the jungles of Sumatra. The rat, big as a tiger, had once glared at the world through bold and cunning emerald eyes. But the gems had been pried out by thieves, leaving the giant rat to wander the seas like a blind man. The ivory teeth had yellowed, but remained bared and sharp as crooked nails—a rat eager to sink its jaws into the throat of the unwary.

The ship had come halfway across the world to this sleepy bay on the Mexican coast of California. What was she doing in San Diego? *The Giant Rat of Sumatra* was a pirate ship, a bold outlaw accustomed to plying her trade from Sumatra to the China Sea.

Standing calmly at the ship's rail, I sniffed the air for some dry scent of the earth out there in the dark. It seemed an eternity since I had set foot on land. I'd already had enough of the sea to last me until my voice finally changed. I was twelve years and ten months old and the ship's cabin boy.

I turned to catch sight of the ship's master as he came sliding down the ratlines. The man took a leap like a tall, big-boned acrobat to the bowsprit. There he peered through the rags of fog and shouted orders in midair. "Steersman! An inch to starboard, if you'll be so kind! This channel is tight as a priest's collar! Aye, that's better, shipmates! Steady!"

He was a large man, but I had noticed how light on his feet he was. Drenched by hours bareheaded in the fog, his coarse black hair glistened like needles. He was as apt to be lending a hand pumping water in the bilge as at his sextant fixing the course. He regarded no job aboard ship as beneath him.

It was clear to me that the ship's master was no stranger to this strange port of call. He knew that a vast bed of seaweed lay near the entrance: He skirted it. He appeared as familiar with the bottom of the bay as with the deep creases in his own hands, weathered under foreign suns.

"God bless my eyesight!" he exclaimed with immense pleasure. The captain had a loud, hearty laugh when he felt like laughing, as he did now. "We've brought our pigs to a fine market, sahibs!" It was a Hindi term of respect he was fond of tossing about the decks. "That's San Diego itself hidin' in the fog dead ahead and about to welcome Captain Gallows back. Aye, I've come home after all these years!" He made a sharp chopping motion with his hand. "Drop the hook!"

With a rattling of its rusty chain, the anchor dropped and found the bottom. The ship swung around like a dog pulled tight on its leash.

As I watched him, I could tell that it amused Captain Gallows to sail under such a foreboding name. He flung out orders in a grab bag of languages while he strode toward his quarters. "Jimmy Pukapuka, be so kind as to fetch up a bucket of whale oil and refill the warning lights. In the fog, we shall want to glow like a ghost, amigo!"

"Aye, Cap'n."

"Calcutta, open our last keg of water. And run up our flag!"

"What flag, Cap'n?" replied the second officer, as broadly muscled as a bull.

"Anything but the skull and crossbones. Mr. Ginger! Post a man on watch! Everyone else turn in. Sleep well, shipmates, for tomorrow you will become gentlemen! Cabin boy! We do have a cabin boy, don't we? I recall fishing one out of the sea months ago. Where is that shipwrecked cabin boy?"

"Here, sir."

"Polish my English boots! I don't intend going ashore tomorrow looking like a beggar."

The deck had almost cleared when I sat myself against a deckhouse to polish the boots. Jimmy Pukapuka, a burly Pacific Islander with swirling tattoos on his cheeks, had carried up a full bucket of whale oil. He was soon finished refilling the port and starboard lanterns, with oil left over in the bucket.

"Catch a wink, Shipwreck, boy," he remarked, hanging up the oil bucket and vanishing belowdecks to his bunk.

It was almost inevitable that the crewmen would call me Shipwreck. I had, after all, been dredged up out of the sea. Boston born, I had been taken aboard a smelly whaling ship by my stepfather, an angry man and a harsh ship's officer. He told me that eleven years was quite old enough to earn my own keep. And a sea voyage would toughen me up for a short-tempered world.

After more'n a year and a half, a short-tempered storm off the Philippines had blown the ship into matchsticks. I had found myself clinging like a barnacle to a splintered oak beam. At the other end, cursing to the skies, hung the one-armed chief mate.

The two of us were plucked from the sea by a fast, nimble ship with the figurehead of a great carved rat. Spouting seawater and sputtering, I remember looking around for my stepfather.

"There is no one alive left floating in this storm," the ship's young captain had told me and briskly turned away as one accustomed to death at sea. I recall raising myself to an elbow, as if to check the raging storm for my relative, and then I fell back, exhausted.

It was days later that I fully grasped my situation. I was alive, but just barely, with nothing of my own but the shirt and breeches that had dried to my salt-crusted skin. What would happen to me? My stepfather, with his disapproving gray eyes, was forever gone. I relieved my grief with a dutiful shrug from time to time. As the weeks passed I realized that I no longer truly missed the man. I felt unburdened.

But what would happen to me, now grown to twelve years and ten months? I'd find that out, day by day. The world was full of surprises, I was discovering, for hadn't I already landed on my feet? The young captain had put me quickly to work running errands as ship's cabin boy. The turbaned second officer, whom everyone called Calcutta, had found me a blue coat with brass buttons that fit except for the sleeves.

"Made in London, that coat was!" he had exclaimed with a certain pride in the quality of the ship's appointments. I had rolled up the cuffs and gone about my duties.

The other survivor, the one-armed man, was all battered face and thundering voice and four-cornered oaths. An experienced mariner, he was pressed into service when the former chief mate vanished one night off the Sandwich Islands. Whether the officer had slipped into the sea or was given an unfriendly kick was a subject of belowdecks gossip.

When I first discovered that I owed my life to a band of murderous pirates, of common sea scum, I was wary and tried to keep a safe distance. But as I came to know the crew, cutthroat by cutthroat, my forebodings diminished. While the men struck me as profoundly ignorant, except for knowing the points of the compass and the direction of the wind, they showed no more greed than I'd seen about the streets of Boston. I wondered if more than two or three of them would qualify as genuine cutthroats.

For their part, the pirates were bedazzled that a twelve-year-old cabin boy could read and write as cunningly as the captain himself. To them, I was a wonder! On occasions I wrote a letter home for Chop Chop, the top-sailman, big as a water buffalo. Or for Trot, the wispy-haired sailmaker. I sensed that the man hadn't a soul to write to, but the pretense had brought a sparkle to his watery eyes. "Look ye, address it to Miss Emilie Trot in Cardiff!" he had insisted in a loud, boasting voice. He was beginning to believe his own lie, it seemed to me, but there was no harm in it and I had scribbled away.

I put away these thoughts and finished polishing the maroon boots. What long legs the captain walked on! The man had the carefree air of a gypsy. All he lacked was a gold ring dangling from his ear.

He'd earned some fame, Calcutta told me, by his sharp nose for the richest cargoes afloat in the Far East—other pirate ships. Maybe it eased his conscience to prey almost entirely on his own kind, I thought—though he seemed prepared to make exceptions.

Now, like a homing pigeon, he had brought his ship to Mexican waters. What would he do tomorrow? Step ashore like a conqueror returning home in maroon English boots?

Finally I left his footgear standing and crossed to the open rail. Peering through the drifting fog, I again hoped to glimpse a treetop or a headland. Maybe San Diego would be the port to find another ship, one bound for New England, thousands of miles away. All I wanted now was to find some way home.

I reached into my pocket for a sea biscuit,

months stale and hard as a bone. I began to gnaw on it. Was this what my stepfather had meant by toughening me up? A near drowning and now sea biscuits! I felt toughened up more than necessary.

Out of a swirl of fog, a heavy hand landed on my shoulder and dug in like a claw.

"What you gazin' at, Shipwreck?"

I looked up sharply. I knew the voice well enough, now set at a whisper at my ear. This was the man who had survived the sinking with me—One-Arm Ginger. Now a ship's officer, Mr. Ginger might not be next to God aboard *The Giant Rat of Sumatra*, but he was next to the captain himself.

"Scurry aft," he commanded. "Lower the flyboat. Not a sound, mind you. It's private business."

"The flyboat? It's hardly big enough for two, sir."

"How am I to row ashore with one arm, I ask ye? Fetch the oars!"

"I've the captain's boots to finish shining."

"You can polish later. Step along before the fog lifts."

I jammed the biscuit in my coat pocket. What strange errand was the chief mate up to, sneaking ashore in the fog?

With the sleeve of his blue coat hanging loose and empty as a gutted fish, the man seated himself opposite me in the nutshell of a boat. I began to row.

"Land's sittin' that way, me lad," the barrel-chested mate said, poking a thick finger through the fog. "Can't you smell the hide houses? It's La Playa, around the bend from the town, stinking just the same as I remember it. It must be five years ago I jumped ship." He cackled softly. "Too lawless for San Diego, is La Playa. Smell it! Aye, it's the stink of cowhides our clever captain can't get out of his high and mighty nose, if you ask me. He's got a score to settle here, from the smolder I seen in his eyes. Row. Row, lad."

I could hear thin sounds of laughter and revelry ashore. I steered toward the distant noise as if it were a compass setting. Soon a lighted window came glowing through the fog, now beginning to fray into black lace.

"Look there!" said One-Arm Ginger with a happy flutter of his eyebrows. "That's me old drink house, matey! The Red Dolphin! And sounds like Sam'l Spoons himself still leadin' the seafarin' choir! I'd know that cacklin' voice if I was stone deaf!"

We pulled up on a wet sandy beach and trudged the few steps to a seaman's tavern with its red wooden sign dripping the night's fog like blood. Flinging the door open, One-Arm Ginger burst through the doorway. For an instant laughter was sucked out of the room. Who was this wild-eyed figure in the middle of the night? The devil himself in brass buttons?

"Don't you know me, lads? It's Ginger himself, about to make each seagoing man of you rich as a king! Is that you, Sam'l Spoons, you old thief? Don't you remember yur old shipmate?"

The barkeep, wearing an apron so dirty he might have been cleaning fish, lifted a lantern for a closer look.

"Ginger! Ain't you been hung once or twice yet? What happened to your arm?"

"Eaten off by piranha fish!"

"Gnawed? Naw!"

Ginger waved his empty sleeve. "Ain't that proof enough?"

"Must have felt a tad unpleasant, matey!" exclaimed the barkeep, crossing himself.

"I was so soaked in black rum I felt hardly a nibble. I woke up the next morning with me arm dangling in the Amazon River, gnawed to the bone, and I been One-Arm Ginger ever since."

In the shadows of the earthen floor, an otter hunter with long greasy hair raised his voice. "If that story's true, I'm stupid, mate!"

Ginger raised a tangled eyebrow. "Then you're stupid, lad! The bottom truth is I'm looking to employ a crew of able-bodied men who won't fret if I make 'em ugly rich. I'll stuff so much gold in yur pockets, both knees'll bend like barrel staves. How about you gents, all three? You there, with your harpoon, is it sharp? Can you strike a barracuda with it?"

"A minnow, sir!" said a short seaman wearing a black neckerchief. "And dance a jig at the same time, can Ozzie Twitch. Not that it's any business of yours!" he added, topping off his reply with a laugh. Then, with his bare feet on the sandy floor, he jumped into a sailor's jig. I saw dead flies stuck to the fresh tar of his seaman's pigtail.

"You'll do," said One-Arm Ginger, his eyes shooting about. "And the rest of you brave lads, you ain't afraid of the hangman's rope, are ye? For we may be sailin' outside the law. If there be an ounce of pesky honesty in your bones, there's the door of the Red Dolphin and it's wide open."

No one stirred. I was uneasy standing there. I didn't like the chief mate's mangy shadow falling across me. What riches was he promising this riffraff? The ship's biscuits? It crossed my mind that my stepfather had drowned with a psalm on his lips while this rogue was plucked from the sea with curses on his. Where was the sense in the senselessness of it?

One-Arm Ginger was grinning. "No one streakin' for the door, I see. You with me, too, Sam'l Spoons?"

"I'm too old for that brand of mischief, brother. This whitewashed adobe is treasure enough for old Sam'l, now I've joined the Mexican nation and become an upstanding Californio."

"You got come over with holiness?" asked One-Arm Ginger contemptuously. "I seen you crossin' yourself every time I pause for breath. I thought you was flea-bit."

"Aye, to own me own land I had to take on a full cargo of the king's own religion. Folks kick you out if you ain't been baptized. Everyone in this bilgewater port goes to Mass except the sea lions and the coyotes." He crossed himself again. "And think how it impresses the natives with me purity, Ginger! You go right ahead with your bloody business and don't mind me. I see you won the loyalty of me guests. As full of greed as their hide'll hold, the lot of 'em."

"Drinks for the house!" commanded One-Arm Ginger with a generous sweep of his hand. "I've found me as fine a set of villains as ever crossed salt water!"

The barkeep shifted his glance to me. "A small portion for the lad? I'll only charge you half."

It was as if the chief mate had forgotten me standing behind him. He turned and his cheeks puffed up. "Who told you to stick to me like a pilot fish, cabin boy?" he asked. "Return to the ship, and when you see Captain Alejandro Gallows himself, give him a salute from me and a respectful thumb of the nose." He burst out a laugh. "Sam'l, give this shipwrecked boy a candlestick to light his way through the fog."

I shook my head. "The fog's lifting. I don't need a candle to find *The Giant Rat*."

"Take the blasted light! Do as you're told!"

An empty bottle with a limp candle plugged into the neck was stuck into my hand. Only then did the man's cleverness flash through my mind. As he watched the candle flame recede in the night, One-Arm Ginger could be assured that I wasn't close by and listening at the window.

I closed the door behind me and hurried through the sand to the flyboat. I looked back and hesitated only a moment. Then I planted the candlestick upright on the wooden seat and pushed the flyboat into the bay. I hardly paused to wonder how I would get back to the ship without it. As the flyboat drifted away I watched the flame glittering like a toe dancer in the night.

Peering back at the Red Dolphin, I wasn't surprised to see the face of One-Arm Ginger pressed against the window. The man's eyes peered into the night: watching the candle flame grow smaller.

Keeping myself low, I crept back to the tavern wall. Once the chief mate's broad face was gone from the window, I raised myself close enough to listen. What bloody venture was One-Arm Ginger hatching inside the tavern? I pressed my ear closer, afraid of what I might hear.

CHAPTER ❖ 3

"*There's* treasure sitting at anchor out in the harbor, lads," said One-Arm Ginger. "Gold coins from India and jewels from China so bright they'll blind yur eyes."

"I'll risk lookin' at a feast like that!" piped up the otter hunter. I caught sight of his face glowing up like a lantern with sudden greed.

"Treasure talk is cheap in these waters," said Ozzie Twitch, the harpooner. "Treasure to the touch is another thing."

"It's there in the captain's own sea chest," replied One-Arm Ginger with a snort. "Didn't I see it with me own eyes? Ain't he been hoarding like a miser through the years? Aye, so he could return here where he was born poor as dirt. Like a fish to his spawning ground, you see, but risen in the world! He'll be taking the longboat ashore at first light to buy himself a hilltop or two. He told me so himself! Aye, quitting the sea, the tall Mexican is, to set himself up like a duke of the realm!"

My breath caught. Was this how the chief mate was going to repay Captain Gallows for fishing him out of the sea? With robbery? With bloody murder?

The harpooner clamped a suspicious eye on One-Arm Ginger. "Why you cutting us in, mate? Born generous, were you? Why split the treasure with sea worms like us?"

One-Arm Ginger flung his fist in the air, almost touching the low ceiling, and pounded it on the bar. "Will you tell me how I can tote that heavy sea chest with one hand? I'll tell you. I'll need the tentacles of an octopus!"

"Then lead the way!" exclaimed the otter hunter. "Tomorrow soon enough?"

"Tonight!" replied One-Arm Ginger sharply. "I posted no man on watch. Tonight we'll steal aboard, silent as mice, and relieve the captain of the burden. A sharp harpoon at his throat ought to tame him."

"Not a pretty way to show your loyalty," remarked the harpooner.

"Treasure is treasure," answered One-Arm Ginger.

At that point, I dropped down from the window. I needed to scurry back to the ship and wake the captain.

I turned to run, and plowed into the arms of the barkeep in his smelly apron.

"I thought I saw white eyes at the window!" Sam'l Spoons declared. "I reckon you got an earful. Don't you know me old shipmate'll wring the breath out of you? Like water from a sponge. Touchy as a marlin spike, is he."

I said nothing. I felt myself wriggling like a caught fish.

"Well, I don't want murder on me doorstep," said the barkeep. "Not good for trade. Come along, quiet now, sonny!"

The barkeep dragged me to a rough wooden door at the back of the tavern. He flung me inside and locked the door.

"I'll let you out before you're full grown, I promise you. Can't let you run off and get your neck wrung, can I?"

I put my back to the wall while a dog began to growl across the pitch dark room. I stiffened. My heart thundered, not in terror for myself so much as in fear for Captain Gallows, about to be croaked in his sleep.

The dog's growling ventured closer. I couldn't pick out the beast, but he could sense my body heat approaching him in the moldy, damp-smelling room. Moving slowly,

I fished the half-gnawed biscuit out of my pocket.

"Dog," I whispered. "Here's some grub for you. A first-rate sea biscuit. Hard as a bone. You got yourself a name? You bite? Smell this."

I waited, frozen. Then I could feel the dog's breath on my hand.

"Be quick about it, dog," I muttered earnestly. "Grub it down and let me find a way out of here."

The dog carried off the biscuit, and a moment later I could hear his teeth grinding away.

"Now, dog, how can I get out of here?"

I felt around in the heavy dark. There seemed nothing in the storeroom but barrels and bottles, an anchor chain, and an oar or two smelling of the sea. I found the door and tried it again. It was locked tight.

As I moved away, I heard the animal scratching away at the earthen floor. Was he burying the bone-hard biscuit? Near the door?

Following the sound, I bumped into the dog. The growling had stopped. I put out a hand to risk petting the animal's back. Woolly as a sheep.

"Easy, mate. Dig if you want to. Maybe you can dig us both out of here."

Only as the words left my mouth did I realize what I'd said. Smart dog!

Like a blind man, arms stretched before me in the dark, I found my way back to the oars.

I chose one, feeling the edge of the paddle. It wasn't a shovel, but it would do.

I felt my way back to the door. "Stand aside, dog."

I dug away as if I were paddling a canoe— for my very life. The hole grew slowly larger. I kept digging away as my mind drifted to the tall captain and the gossip I'd heard in my fo'c'sle bunk.

The crew believed he'd fallen into the trade of piracy by accident. While hardly older than me, he'd served aboard a ship in the China trade. He had been taken prisoner aboard *The Giant Rat of Sumatra* and put to work bailing out the bilge. Before he was twenty, with a commanding boldness and a quick wit, he had raised himself to the position of second and then chief mate. When the ship's master had the carelessness to get himself hung from a Hong Kong gallows, the young chief mate was elected captain and assumed a new name. Captain Gallows! "Aye," Calcutta had remarked, "the name honored our old master, left hanging aloft as a perch for the bewildered Hong Kong harbor seagulls!"

I kept measuring the enlarging hole with the blade of the oar. Moments later I could no longer hear the dog grinding away on the biscuit. Had he slipped out?

He had!

I fell to my stomach. I pulled myself into the hole, arms out, and squeezed myself into the night.

I jumped around to the window, hoping to glimpse One-Arm Ginger still there, flailing his hand in the air and scheming. But too much time had passed. The tavern had fallen silent.

The assassins were already afoot.

I turned and ran for the waterline.

CHAPTER ❖ 4

DESPERATE EVENTS ABOARD THE GIANT RAT
AND A BUCKET OF WHALE OIL

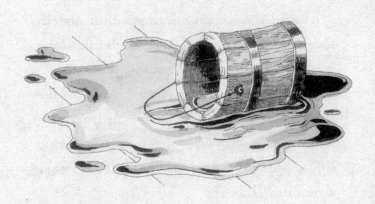

I could see the foggy glow of the port
lantern on *The Giant Rat of Sumatra* at
anchor in the bay. And I thought I could
make out a longboat slipping like a ghost
through the darkness.

I wished now I hadn't sent the flyboat

floating on the tide. How was I going to sound the alarm? I cast my eyes about but saw no sign of a flickering stub of a candle. Perhaps it had burned itself out.

I heard a voice thundering within myself. Captain Gallows is asleep in his bunk! Can't you swim to the ship? That far?

I remembered the oar left behind in the storeroom. If Sam'l Spoons owned oars, he must own a boat. Would that be a boat making soft lapping sounds on the tide? Farther around the shore?

I followed my ears. Tucked behind a shallow bend I found a rowboat tethered like a goat to an iron stake in the earth. The oarlocks stood empty. Of course, I thought! The barkeep kept the oars from being stolen.

I tried not to lose any more time than I had to. I rushed with sandy shoes back to the rear of the tavern. I crawled back under the door and was quick to discover one oar and then the other.

I worked them under the door and out.

Soon I had them in the boat's oarlocks and shoved off into the bay.

As I scraped the hull of *The Giant Rat of Sumatra,* its side lanterns lit, I knew I was too late. An oaken longboat was already tied to the jack ladder. It waited quietly for the attackers to return and flee.

I untied the longboat and shoved it away to drift free. I climbed hand over hand up the jack ladder, not sure now what I could do except to wake the crew. How calculating of the chief mate to have posted no man on watch!

But once I reached the deck, the hatch doors flew open and out backed One-Arm Ginger himself, a knife flashing in his hand. Beside him came the harpooner, the long handle of his weapon broken off.

I acted on instinct. My attention was quickly drawn to the bucket of whale oil Jimmy Pukapuka had left hooked to the deckhouse.

I grabbed the bucket. It was still heavy and,

mercifully, half full. That would do! I splashed the whale oil on deck. It landed in a great puddle near the feet of the villains as they came backing out of the hatch, flailing away with their weapons.

"Fools! Dolts! Chaff and bran!" came the captain's booming voice. "Sea worms! I'll send you headlong into eternity!" He appeared now, a tall, grinning Mexican with a jungle knife in his fist and bookish words flying from his lips. The blade, as broad as a bed slat, flashed like lightning, backing the men out of the hatch.

I saw with a rush of relief that the captain was very much alive and on his feet. He seemed to be enjoying himself hugely.

But quickly the captain was forced to back away. The three ruffians advanced on him, knives and harpoon whipping the air. The fight disappeared into the hatch. I froze, my heart pounding.

Moments later, the doors of the hatch again flew open, but now it was Captain

Gallows backing into the night. The assassins were driving him out on deck.

"You've trifled with my good nature and the laws of mutiny, Mr. Ginger!" shouted the captain defiantly. "I'll be obliged to hoist you and your fellows from the yardarms! I shall hang you up like soiled laundry!"

"Blast yur eyes, sir!" shouted One-Arm Ginger.

"Fight on, *cucarachas*! I have stepped on more menacing cockroaches!"

To my horror, I saw the captain take a long backward step. As he slipped on the oiled deck, his legs flew from under him. He ripped out oaths in several languages.

The scoundrels were quick to rush on the fallen captain with their blades hoisted in the air.

But their legs, too, went spinning.

The ship rolled in the tide, and the four men went slithering toward the open railing. Setting my feet firmly against a deck cleat, I caught the captain's bare brown arm and held tight.

One-Arm Ginger, now as oily as a sardine,

slipped over the side. He flopped into the sea
with hardly a splash and only a gasp of surprise. Clinging to him, the harpooner followed, and then the otter hunter, his long
hair flying.

"Who in thunder spilled oil on deck!" the
captain shouted, clinging to me as if I were a
solid post. He carefully steadied himself on
his slippery feet.

"I thought they were going to finish you
off, sir," I answered. "I meant only to tangle
their feet with whale oil."

The captain cocked a black eyebrow. "Did
you, Shipwreck? That was lively thinking."
And then with a shout, "Where in blazes is
the man on watch? Who let that sea scum
aboard?"

"Mr. Ginger didn't post a watchman, sir. I
heard him say so."

"Sly rascal."

"Yes, sir."

"Must I call you Shipwreck, cabin boy? Do
you have a proper name?"

"Shipwreck'll do."

"Shipwreck, I'm obliged to you."

I felt a glow of pride in myself. I was glad to please this man who had plucked me from the high seas.

The scuffling on deck was bringing a few sleepy seamen on deck.

Said the captain, "You, Jimmy Pukapuka, stick your head over the side and see if any of those sea vultures can swim, which is unlikely. The rest of you, dredge up buckets of seawater and wash down the deck, before we all follow the nitwits over the side."

Jimmy Pukapuka gazed over the side and finally announced, "Nothing down there, Cap'n. Only a sea lion enjoyin' his guests."

Captain Gallows waved in his crew. "Lower your chins, shipmates. Anyone want to say a few solemn words for these muckworms and murderers? No? Padre, have mercy on their souls, but lock up your silver candlesticks. Amen."

At the break of dawn, Captain Gallows sent the remaining longboat ashore for fresh water and galley supplies from among the hide houses. Now that it was light, I could see what appeared to be an abandoned fort at the headland. Closer in stood the ramshackle warehouses of La Playa, with stiff cowhides folded and piled like the weathered pages of old books. Around the bend, San Diego seemed to be keeping the scruffy place at arm's length.

The second officer, Calcutta, who had seen the world several times over, told me the hides would be shipped to Boston and return as leather shoes and boots for the Californios. Other hides would be traded in China and India for silks and ivory and perfumes and porcelain dishes.

"See San Diego, around the bay?" said Calcutta, pointing a stubby finger. "You could put that dusty town itself in a bird's nest, but don't be fooled, lad. San Diego is captain of the hide trade. Important as London town, if you're a cow!" And the second officer laughed.

As soon as I could, I rowed ashore, finding Sam'l Spoons asleep on the counter and snoring thunderbolts.

"Thanks for the borrow of your boat," I

muttered, being careful not to disturb the barkeep.

The dog was off in a corner, asleep, too.

But *The Giant Rat's* flyboat was floating like driftwood on the incoming tide. Soon I was able to wade out knee-deep in the water to reclaim it and row to the ship. That's when the longboat came in sight again, this time with Captain Gallows standing at the stern, one polished maroon boot resting on a sea chest. His eyes surveyed the few adobe buildings farther around the bay that called themselves San Diego.

Now that the pirates had reached their destination, I realized that I was finished with *The Giant Rat of Sumatra*. I could see three ships at anchor in the bay. By thunder, one of them might be setting its course for the long voyage around South America to New England. And I'd be home, at last!

It was now more than twenty-one months since I had left my actress mother standing under her orange parasol on India Wharf in

Boston. Had word trickled back that my stepfather had drowned? How could she guess
that I had survived, shipwrecked but floating? It seemed a lifetime ago that I was an
eleven-year-old with my head buried in the
collar of my new coat while my stepfather
dragged me aboard the doomed whaler. I
couldn't get my mother's festive orange parasol out of my mind. Shouldn't it have been a
sad black for the occasion? Falling asleep
night after night in my fo'c'sle bunk, I would
wonder why she hadn't balked at letting me
be carried off to sea. I recalled being homesick before the ship left the wharf. Was she
glad to get me out from underfoot? The
parasol was all smiles. I wasn't sure that she
had liked having a child to look after. Well, I
didn't need looking after anymore.

It was hours before Captain Gallows
returned to the ship. From the way the boat
crew lifted it, the captain's sea chest was now
light as a gourd.

"Amigos!" he called out. "On deck! You

company of scoundrels! I said I would make gentlemen of you, and I shall!"

The bewildered pirates gathered around the mainmast. As I had never come to feel that I belonged to their company, I climbed a rope ladder apart from the others to listen.

"Look you, mates," the captain said, stroking his jaw. "You have served this voyage well. Did you grumble to leave our pirate waters? Shall I remind you that five nations were seeking to hang you together like a bunch of grapes from the nearest gallows? Amigos! These waters are safe. Go ashore. If you dab your faces with fresh water, you might even be seen to be human."

"The last time I washed me face, Cap'n, it shocked me out of a year's growth!" said Bajo, the cook, laughing. "I didn't know I was that no-account ugly!"

The captain grinned. "When we shared out our accounts off Sumatra, you spent every copper the day we docked in Singapore. When we shared out again, you lavished your spoils on Hong Kong. In Manila, your purses were full and lumpy, but I have kept you aboard to preserve you from yourselves. The time has come to cock an eye at our profession. We are at the end of our sea road, shipmates! We have been all but swept off the oceans of the world. Our hunting grounds have shrunk to a few trifling seas in the Far East! Gentlemen, we are as out-of-date as the longbow!"

"God preserve us all!" exclaimed Jimmy Pukapuka.

Said Calcutta, "Don't talk like my mossy old bones are ready for the boneyard, Cap'n."

"And me not yet twenty!" chimed in Jimmy Pukapuka. "Finished, says you?"

The captain took a breath. "You lads have brought *The Giant Rat of Sumatra* to our last port of call. Her eyes have been gouged out. The sails hang in rags. Her ship's bottom is crawling with sea worms. The time has come to gather up your trinkets and abandon ship."

"Upon my conscience," muttered Trot, the barefooted sailmaker. "Can't we patch her up?"

"The patches already have patches," said Captain Gallows.

"But only six or eight times over," remarked Calcutta. "There's still life in this seagoing old rodent, Cap'n."

Captain Gallows shook his head. "You may linger aboard until you find another berth. There is a hide ship loading nearby where I have found you honest employment—if you are tempted by the novelty of that brand of work. Or you may join me ashore. I have already arranged to buy a great rancho and a thousand head of cattle."

"Turning your back on the sea?" exclaimed Trot in open-eyed amazement. "Strike me dead! What are you going to do with all them cows?"

"I shall become a hidalgo."

"What in tarnation is that?"

The captain answered with a snort and a

laugh. "A title reserved for a full-rigged gentleman—whether he is one or not."

"I declare," said Trot, wiping his neck with a rag.

"And I declare that you seagoing men can fling a rope like a vaquero on horseback," the captain continued. "You are welcome to join me and put earth between your toes."

A few of the buccaneers, including Jimmy Pukapuka and Trot and Calcutta, volunteered to stick with the captain and become gentlemen of sorts.

I found myself peering at the ship loading up nearer shore. Like a trail of ants, men were carrying aboard cowhides dried and folded over poles. Was the ship bound for Atlantic waters? There might be room aboard for a cabin boy.

The voyage home would take months. I could hardly expect my mother to know me as I came bursting through the door. The sun had roasted me brown as a coconut, and my hair had bleached like so much straw. I must have grown two or three inches.

The captain was talking again. "They tell me ashore that there is trouble in Mexico. I must warn any of you men who wish to jump ship here and go your own way—foreigners are viewed with suspicion. Especially Americans. Mercifully, none of you are Americans, eh?"

I stiffened a little. What did Mexico have against Americans? I waited for the captain to pause for breath, and called out, "That hide ship, sir. Heading out for New England, if I'm lucky?"

"Bound for Canton."

I gave a disappointed sigh. China. I sat on a yardarm, my legs dangling free. I'd have to turn up another passage home. How long would that take? Again, there flashed across my mind that picture of my mother with her garden-party orange parasol seeing me off in Boston for a dangerous life at sea. How could she have been sure I'd be back?

"Shipwreck!"

"Aye?"

"Pack up your things," said Captain Gallows.

"Everything I own is in my pockets, sir. All my old life drowned."

Had the captain forgotten that he had dredged me out of the sea?

"I will confer with you in my quarters," said Captain Gallows.

*T*he captain's cabin stretched the width of the ship, with aft windows set at a slant and overlooking the water. I stood at the door and cleared my throat.

"I forgot," the captain said, not bothering to notice me. "You said you were an American. Come in."

I stepped through the doorway. A breeze was blowing through the cabin, and it smelled of seaweed.

"So what shall I do with you, American? Are you homesick?"

"A little."

"Only a little? I was never homesick."

"Yes, sir."

"I was once a cabin boy."

I said nothing.

"Amazed, eh? Every proud and noisy frog was once a pollywog. San Diego has always had the hide trade, ships coming and going, so it was easy for me to run away to sea. I was only a little older than you. My first voyages were to China. Then to England. It was a hen ship."

I had heard about hen ships. It meant the captain had kept his wife aboard.

"That grand lady saw a spark in me and decided to teach me to read and write. When we got to London, she put me in school. Don't I talk like Shakespeare himself?"

The captain burst out laughing. I found it

difficult to look up. I couldn't imagine why the ship's master was telling me all this. Or how the man had gone from Shakespeare to piracy.

As if reading my mind, Captain Gallows leaned forward and lowered his voice. "Don't wonder what I am doing aboard *The Giant Rat of Sumatra*. I will tell you. It is difficult to be a poor Mexican. So I became a rich Mexican."

I didn't know whether to smile or let the remark go by me. Was the captain so exalted that he didn't have anyone aboard he could talk to? Was that the way it was with ships' masters, who held the power of gods? Talking to a cabin boy was talking to thin air, wasn't it? Did he really care what I thought of him?

"I detected a spark in you," continued the tall Mexican. "It appears that you are going to find yourself beached in this sleepy pueblo for a while. Leave that to me. If I were to have you taught to read and write—just imagine! You might grow up to be another Captain Gallows."

"I can already read and write, sir."

"Blimey, is there nothing left remarkable

beneath the visiting moon?" he exclaimed. It struck me as something he'd got out of a book. Was that what Shakespeare sounded like? "But you still have the misfortune to be an American."

Captain Gallows began pacing the cabin, ducking his head to avoid the lantern hung from the ceiling. "The news ashore is that Mexico is at war."

I stood unmoved, looking up at the captain. I was sorry that there was a war, but what had that to do with me? Soon I'd find a passage home.

"We are at war with the United States," the captain added.

My gaze faltered. *With the United States.* Did that mean at war with me, Edmund Amos Peters? And how near was the war? There were certainly no cannons booming over this quiet San Diego bay.

"News travels slowly," remarked Captain Gallows. "Fighting began weeks ago. It has not yet reached here."

"Why would Mexico attack the United States?"

"Spoken like a patriot! But it is the United States that has invaded Mexico." The captain turned and bent to stare out the stern windows. "You won't see any ships out there flying your flag. This is a Mexican port. Trade with Boston has stopped. As the devil would have it, Shipwreck, you are not going to find a passage home."

My heart tightened. My plans were turning to ashes. I could think of nothing to do but stare at my feet. How long was I going to be stuck in this confounded Mexican village?

"You may be regarded as an enemy foreigner," said the captain. "War is bound to breed suspicion and craziness. I am told that a militia is forming to battle the Americans. I think you'd better stick close to me, eh, amigo?"

Enemy foreigner? I was too dumbfounded to speak. I felt a little frightened. Couldn't I escape somehow to the United States? How far was it? A thousand miles? Two? Where was it? Beyond Texas somewhere? Too far to walk!

"Meanwhile, you can do me a great service," said the captain. "Ashore they tell me that the law has broken down. Around every bend in the road there is another bandit or cutthroat. My rancho lies almost half a day's ride north of here. I am going to trust you with a great secret. I will be traveling with something of amazing value. Look."

Suddenly, as if he had plucked them out of thin air, the captain held large green stones between the fingers of each hand. They flashed and glowed like cold stars.

"Shipwreck! Do you know what these are?"

I stared at the stones. I knew nothing about gems, except that they were bright and flashing. "Green rocks."

"Trashy rocks, eh? Ah, but what trash! These are emeralds! Two of them, fat as walnuts! Gaze at them, cabin boy. Can you guess where they came from?"

"I think so."

"Tell me."

"The eyes of the giant rat."

"Exactly!" the captain exclaimed. "How cunning of the captain before me! He told everyone they were mere bits of glass. What safer way to protect them from thieves, yes? But no sparkling stones could fool the eyes of a waterfront thief in Hong Kong, who gouged them out. Behold, lad, you are indeed gazing at the stolen eyes of *The Giant Rat of Sumatra*!"

I looked at them again. They seemed to flash lights of their own in the cabin shadows, like the lightning bugs I remembered in Boston.

A smile flickered across the captain's face. "I had hardly been the ship's master a year when word reached me that a Malay thief was trying to sell a pair of great emeralds across the water in Macao. We set sail, and I found him. I might have strangled the scoundrel on the spot, but he had a wife and three children with him. What could I do? So I bought the gems, fair and square, with gold from my private account, and they became mine, no? It's these green treasures, worth a ship's cargo, that our one-armed friend Mr. Ginger, got wind of and came after. Whether others in my crew have similar schemes, I cannot guess. But these green eyes are no longer safe in a pouch around my neck, eh? They will be safer in your hands."

I was startled. "Mine?"

"Who will suspect there is anything of value in the possession of a cabin boy? No one!"

I shook my head. "No, sir. I lose things!"

"Like what?"

"Didn't I almost lose my life?"

The captain playfully lifted an eyebrow. "But your life was a trifle. These are emeralds!"

"What if I run away with them!"

"Run where? You are trapped, you know. I will have to trust you."

I looked again at the gems. Those two confounded stones in my pocket were going to weigh a ton. Then I gave a shrug. "Well, if I lose them, it'll be your funeral."

"No, shipmate, it will be your funeral."

With a sailmaker's needle, the captain sewed the emeralds into the bottom hem of my baggy blue coat. Only after I left the cabin did I pause to realize that Captain Gallows had shown uncommon courtesy. He had not once reminded me that I owed a thundering great favor—*The Giant Rat of Sumatra* had troubled to pluck me from the sea. I could trouble myself to walk around with a fortune in gems in the hem of my coat.

*T*he captain's rancho spread from the sea cliffs to the bright mustard haze of foothills rising to the east. Together with a stout city official in a black frock coat and dusty boots, the captain stood on the cliff top studying an ink-drawn map of the property.

Waiting with Trot and Pukapuka, I watched from the nearby shade of the rambling adobe house, abandoned and silent. The men came armed for trouble on the roads with knives and wooden belaying pins from the ship. I tried to ignore the emeralds lurking in my coat, but they felt as bulky as cannonballs.

"Everything correct?" asked the official, blowing dust off his glasses. I didn't know who he was exactly, but he looked important.

"The property seems unnecessarily vast, Señor Machado."

"Yes," the official replied with a chuckle. "Our misfortune is that there is so much cactus land in California that the governor has trouble giving it away. The moment this rancho was available, I petitioned for it in your name."

"What happened to the owner?"

"Colonel Roberto, the Englishman? *Caramba*, his own Indians had turned on him. Another of the Indian rebellions. Everyone is in a temper these days. And him a loyal citizen of Mexico. We had almost forgotten he was an Englishman. And you? You cannot receive a grant of land if you are not a man of Mexico. Your letters assured me, sir—"

"The mission will have my records. I was brought here as a child on orders from the viceroy of Mexico himself. That should qualify me."

"Ah, yes, the poor orphans, given away like unwanted puppies. You have risen in the world, Captain!"

"You have not used my true name?"

"You have not revealed it to me, sir. The grant is in the name of Captain Alejandro Gallows."

"That will serve."

"You understand you must live in this house, this hacienda, standing on your grant? And you must stock your land with cattle to hold your title?"

"I have already deposited funds with Judge Bomba, my agent of many years, to buy three thousand head of cattle."

"So great a herd to start?" replied Señor Machado. "You will make Don Simplicio himself jealous, may the fleas of a thousand dogs live in his beard."

"I remember the man well," said the captain with a cold shrug.

The official straightened his round shoulders. "Now you must throw stones into the four winds and declare that you are taking possession of El Rancho del Soledad."

Captain Gallows scratched around in the dirt until he had found stones to his liking. Then, as hard as he could throw, he cast one north, one east, then south and west. With a small, private smile, he said, "I take possession of El Rancho Candalaria."

"So?" remarked Señor Machado, making a note. "Named for your wife, Captain?"

The captain did not answer. The seamen and I looked at one another. If the tall Mexican had a wife, he had kept it a secret aboard ship.

The official smiled and shut his soiled

book of documents. "The land is yours, Captain Gallows! Watch out for horse thieves, mountain lions, Americans, bandits, fleas, Indians—and your fellow Mexicans. *Suerte.*"

"Luck?" replied the captain, smiling. "I prefer to make my own."

The men led their rented horses to the well and began to fill the dry horse trough.

I poked around the abandoned ranch house. Here and there a small lizard scurried out of the way, like dust come to life. I paused to look through the window openings. Thieves had evidently carried off everything they could carry, including the window glass. The rooms were bare and lifeless, with walls a foot thick. What was the captain going to do with so many empty rooms, I wondered? One could get lost.

For the moment, it was good to feel solid land under my feet again and even to sniff dust in the air.

I found myself watching the waves as they flung themselves uselessly against the cliffs.

They burst like pottery. Same as me, I thought, rushing eastward but stopped by these infernal Mexican cliffs.

A sound inside the house caught my ear. Did a door slam? I turned and looked down the long veranda that ran along the south side of the house. I wondered if I had just heard the sea wind banging a door, but I went inside the house to look around.

I glanced at the white stuccoed kitchen and the adjoining rooms. Cobwebs hung like wispy ghosts from the ceiling beams. As I wandered along the gritty plank floors, room to room, I saw that my shoes were leaving footprints in the dust. And that's when I saw other footprints. Smaller ones.

Someone was in the house.

Someone in bare feet.

I opened another door and peered into a room with a shelfload of books scattered to the floor, evidently tossed aside as useless to the thieves. Footprints led my eyes to a pile of rubble where part of the roof had caved in.

The cobwebs looked as if they had been roughly swept aside.

As I approached, a figure trailing cobwebs rose like a jack-in-the-box from the fallen roof tiles. I fell back astounded, as if confronted by a real ghost. But it was a girl and very much alive. She was yelling like something untamed and frightened. *"Aieee! Aieee!"*

She burst past me, her bare feet flying. She was wearing a rag of a red dress and shell bracelets. Like a surprised mouse, she was out the door and gone almost before I could get over my astonishment. She was shrieking in panic.

I rushed after her.

With the same sudden amazement, the captain and his men turned to see the girl as she burst outside. They spread out to stop her, but she dodged one and then another.

It would have been easier to catch a wild animal. Pukapuka waved his tattooed arms wide to block her way. She darted under them, her eyes flaring white and terrified.

"Asesinos! Asesinos!" she was yelling.

What was she screaming, I wondered? It sounded like assassins. Assassins?

"Quiet, child!" commanded the captain. "No one is going to murder you!"

The men closed in and trapped her. The captain began talking to her in Spanish. She interrupted, *"Asesinos!"*

She flung out her hands as if to strike him, went limp, and fainted. Captain Gallows caught her. He picked her up and turned to carry her out of the sun and back into the house.

That's when I saw a small Indian woman wrapped in a shawl standing near the wall. She extended her arms. The captain shook his head and carried the girl into the kitchen.

I watched as the captain and the Indian woman talked rapidly in Spanish. The girl came to and wrapped herself in a tight ball. The woman, who later turned out to be her aunt, managed to calm her.

It was clear enough that they had been living

in the deserted house, hiding from murderers and assassins. The captain told them that they could safely stay there. He offered to hire them and any other Indians who might be hiding. He intended to bring the rancho quickly back to life.

On the ride back to San Diego, he recounted what the older woman had told him in Spanish. "A rumor had sprung up that the Indians on the rancho were planning an uprising. There were sixty or seventy of them. They would kill the Englishman and steal all his cattle and sheep. *Dios mio!* Someone did. She crossed herself a dozen times to tell me it wasn't the Indians. But tempers caught fire among the Californios. They began hunting the Indians like wild animals. These revolts and chases have happened before. The young girl, who was eleven, and her aunt had survived at first by hiding in the ocean waves. Then they crept into the house. They've been hiding there since last winter."

The captain turned his head to make sure

that I was following close behind on one of his rented horses. "Don't let that beast run away with you. Have you ever ridden a horse before?"

"No, sir."

"Hold the reins higher. Tighter."

I saw that the captain was keeping me always in the corner of his eye. The jewels had shackled us together.

CHAPTER • 8

*I*n the town plaza, two ragged soldiers from the old Spanish presidio on the hill were attempting to drill seven young men into a militia. The marching about only served to make me aware that the country was at war and that I was the enemy. I reminded myself not to open my American mouth in public, even though I was hearing English spoken everywhere.

Captain Gallows turned to me as if he could sense what I was thinking. "Aye, you Americans!" he said playfully, but with a touch of scorn. "Your Boston ships hold the foreign trade in the palms of your hands. And we are a trading port. So we were obliged to learn your language. You see, it is all your fault, Shipwreck!" The captain burst out laughing.

I gave back a skin-deep smile.

"When I was a boy you could hear English from San Diego to San Francisco," the captain continued. "If we lose this war, our tongues will hardly notice the difference!"

"Do you expect to lose?"

"Why not? Look at those men marching. Do you call that an army? The government in Mexico City is far, far away. They sent us what kind of soldiers? Convicts, most of them! When I was a boy, they raided everyone's gardens. Fight a war with what? Stolen figs? The capital has always looked at us as a curse and a burden, like barnacles on a ship."

My gaze returned to the militia marching under the full blaze of the sun. The soldiers might be convicts, but the young men looked enthusiastic and determined. I felt a certain safety in staying within the protection of Captain Gallows's long Mexican shadow.

"And you," he said suddenly. "What do I know about you? You have the look of an orphan."

"No, sir."

"It was your father who drowned, no?"

"Stepfather. My father was an actor."

"And your mother?"

"On the stage, too."

"To have a mother is a celebration," said Captain Gallows.

I gave a shrug. Maybe. I hoped so.

"And now you have begun life of your own, eh?" continued the captain. "That, too, is a celebration."

"Is it?"

"What will you make of it?"

I shrugged.

"The wide world is waiting for you."

I shrugged again. What was out there for me?

He broke into a smile. "Of course it is! I think the world is scratching its head at this very minute and wondering what it will make of that half-drowned boy, Shipwreck. Be patient, cabin boy. You will find out!"

I nodded and felt like smiling. "Maybe I'll become a pirate like you?"

"You think I am flattered? Shipwreck, I was born to set a bad example. If I find you in my footsteps, I will throw you back in the sea!"

We pulled up at a large whitewashed store and stables facing the bay. A huge and prickly clump of cactus stood in front like a dusty armed guard.

I was glad to get off the horse. I was sore and tender, and my first steps hurt. I noticed Captain Gallows rubbing his back as if it had turned to pig iron.

The storekeeper came out to meet us. He included me in his first, friendly glance. He turned out to be Judge Bomba, justice of the peace. Shorter than Captain Gallows by inches, he wore a linen suit and a stand-up collar. He had smiling eyes.

"Judge," said the captain. "Did you make it known that I have deposited funds in your heavy safe to buy cattle?"

"I have already found you five hundred head. Good, scrawny California cows. A hundred sheep. And fifty hogs. Shall I keep buying?"

The captain nodded and grinned. "Tell me, what is Don Simplicio paying for cowhides?"

"That old miser? May the fleas of two thousand dogs—"

"Never mind the vermin. What is he paying?"

"Two dollars."

"Let it be known that I will pay four dollars."

"Each hide?"

"Each."

"Have you been dining on loco weed? Did something drive you crazy, my friend?"

"Make it known. The crazy sea captain is

paying double for hides. Though make it known I will not do business with Don Simplicio Emilio Charro."

I found myself paying closer attention. I understood nothing about trade, but I could see that the captain would be taken for a thundering fool. The tall Mexican appeared unconcerned.

"Don Simplicio Emilio Charro will have fits," said the justice. "He will be forced to pay the same figure to buy hides. I have heard he is in debt."

"Unfortunate fellow," snapped Captain Gallows.

"*Sí.* His last two ships vanished in the China Sea. Pirates, they say. Full cargoes of hides and candles! And a third ship is missing."

"Sunk, too, I can assure you. And Don Simplicio's tallow candles are worthless—too limp to stand under their own flame. The sea rovers did the world a good service."

"Buccaneers!" The storekeeper snorted and clicked his tongue as rapidly as castanets.

"You are fortunate to have escaped the sea swine. They will ruin Don Simplicio."

"I pity the poor fleas. They must be starving in his bloodless chin," said Captain Gallows scornfully, and changed the subject. "Is it still customary when a trade ship anchors in the bay to put on a great ball for the townspeople?"

"Of course. It is our chief entertainment, especially if you have goods to sell. And how our young women dress up!"

"I have a cargo of China silks and porcelain dishes and even spices from Sumatra."

"Splendid, Captain! We are in need of a festival, with this shirttail war on our hands."

"Tomorrow?"

"So soon?"

"Will you oblige me by spreading the word?"

"Believe me," said Judge Bomba. "It will spread itself."

"What about musicians?"

"I will arrange it. Is there room on your ship for dancing?"

"We will make space on the quarterdeck."

"Then it is settled," declared the justice, smiling in anticipation.

"And perhaps you can recommend a *mayordomo*."

"A foreman? For the ship's ball?"

"For the Rancho Candalaria."

The judge paused and closed one eye thoughtfully. "Have you never forgotten that girl? That child? I wrote you, no one remembers her."

"I do," replied Captain Gallows, and quickly changed the subject. "I will need a *mayordomo*. To hire cooks and corn grinders and gardeners and weavers and candlemakers and vaqueros to work with the cattle. Someone to take charge. Someone to bring my hacienda back to life—quickly. In a week."

"A week! No *mayordomo* can do that!"

"Five days would be even better."

"Impossible," said the judge, and then added, running a finger inside his stuff collar, "unless Juan Largo cares to give up shooting horses. He is capable. He is in the store buying beans and sugar. Ask him yourself."

Captain Gallows looked doubtful. "He shoots horses?"

"Wild horses. *Sí.* They have become pesky as crows and eat the grass out from under the grazing cows. So the ranches hired Juan Largo to thin out the wild ones. He is unhappy at the job."

"Long John?" muttered the captain. "I think I remember him."

At that moment, to the jingle of his silver spurs, a man with a weeping-willow mustache walked out of the store. He carried a large sack of beans across his shoulder. He had legs as long and thin as a stork's.

"Juan Largo!" shouted the justice of the peace. "You once did service as Don Simplicio's *mayordomo.* Meet the sea captain, who has a preposterous offer to make."

O" the night of the ball, but while it was still light, Captain Gallows transformed himself. He unpacked Mexican clothing tailored for him in Hong Kong. When he stepped out of his cabin, I hardly recognized him. Silver buttons ran down the sides of his pants. His dark jacket was a swirl of embroidered gold. A silver pistol was stuck under a wide green sash around his waist and his bemused eyes were shaded by a wide-brimmed tan leather hat. "Behold!" he said to his crew. "Today I become Don Alejandro, eh?"

"Whatever you say, Cap'n," remarked Calcutta.

"Have the silks and dishes and spices been laid out for sale? You will be in charge. Chop Chop, did you sprinkle beach sand on the quarterdeck for dancing?"

"In a minute, Don Alejandro."

Trot was still gazing at the transformed captain. "Sir, is it proper to ask a lady to dance with a bloody pistol in your belt?"

"The bloody pistol is for the head of any pirate on deck who utters a bilgewater oath with visitors aboard."

"Gosh!" exclaimed Jimmy Pukapuka.

A boatload of musicians was the first to arrive. The men struggled with their instruments up the ship's rope ladder. They began to play at once, giving the first guests a festive welcome of fiddles and trumpet.

I watched from the mainmast ratlines as Don Alejandro, the silver pistol gone from his sash, welcomed whole boatloads of townspeople. It was Don Boniface this and Doña Victoria that and Señorita something else.

"Imagine!" I heard a man say, gesturing with a gold-headed cane at the bowsprit. "A trading ship with a rat for a figurehead! How curious. How mysterious are these ships from the Spice Islands!"

His companion replied, "Don Antonio, where in the world is Sumatra?"

I heard names. Bandini children chased Carrillo children around the decks and the Mexican governor himself, Pio Pico, pretended to catch them. Judge Bomba said, "Is it true, Governor, that on your rancho nearby you live in a house with nineteen rooms?"

"A lie!" exploded the governor, who then burst into a laugh. "There are twenty-two! I have many relatives!"

Soon the decks were crowded with chattering guests, who seemed overjoyed to escape their ranches for the excitement of the city. The younger men wore vests decorated with spiderwebs of gold and silver thread to match their bell-like trouser cuffs. The women, in swirling skirts and wearing saucy feathers in their hats, were drawn to the dancing or to the cargo of China silks.

I had never laid eyes on a costume ball, but I'd read about them. I'd supposed this was as close as I could expect to come to such fairy-tale happenings. And then it crossed my mind not to forget that I was an enemy alien. I told myself to keep my American voice still. If I had to speak, I would confine my answers to *sí* and *no*—especially in the presence of the governor. He appeared to be seeking relief from the war in a shipboard fiesta.

But my resolve almost gave way when I looked down from the ratlines as a big, coarse-looking man came aboard with his wife. I heard the man's name—Captain Henry Fitch.

Fitch? That was an English name. And his heavy, booming voice sounded American! Why didn't the Mexican authorities have him in manacles? Moving overhead, from rat-lines to shrouds, I followed the man. His wife, as slim as a hummingbird, wanted to join the dancing on the quarterdeck.

"I'm too clumsy for that nonsense," he protested as Captain Gallows approached. "You, young feller, dance with my wife."

"I shall be delighted, Captain Fitch."

"You know who I am?"

"Doesn't everyone? A former sea captain yourself, the first American to make his home in San Diego, and by reputation an honest trader who knows everyone. And this is your charming wife Doña Josefa, one of Joaquin Carrillo's beautiful daughters."

The older man's eyes narrowed. "Who are you, sir?"

"What does it matter? I should like to ask you a question."

"I should like to dance," said Doña Josefa.

"Listen to the trumpet!"

Said Captain Gallows, unwilling to be distracted by a trumpet in the sea air, "Perhaps you recall a girl from long ago, a girl named Candalaria. About twelve years old."

"There are many Candalarias."

"Not in San Diego. She was an orphan."

"Her last name might help, sir."

"She never told me," replied Captain Gallows.

"No?"

"I'm not sure she knew it herself."

"Ask Don Simplicio," advised the older man. "He was forever taking in orphans."

"Don Simplicio does not answer his mail."

"Perhaps that wrinkled old rogue has been dead all these years and is keeping it a secret from us!" Captain Fitch let out a booming laugh, and Don Alejandro accompanied the trader's wife to the dance floor.

I gave my head a slow tilt. It was now clear to me why Captain Gallows was so anxious to throw this party. Someone among the townspeople was bound to remember a twelve-year-old Candalaria. *The Giant Rat of Sumatra* had crossed the Pacific Ocean so that the captain could track her down.

"You up there!"

It was a moment before I realized that someone was yelling at me.

"You! In the yards!"

It was Captain Fitch shouting up at me.

"*Sí*," I said.

"Why are you following me around? Think I'm blind?"

"*No*," I answered.

"What do you want?"

I retreated without another word through the shrouds and lines. When I banged my hand on a turnbuckle, I couldn't help letting out a yelp. "Ouch!"

I kept on my way and slipped through the fo'c'sle hatch. I tumbled down the ladder belowdecks to the safety of my bunk.

I pulled up sharply. I saw a stocky figure stretched out on my bunk.

I'd seen the man before. In the Red Dolphin. The harpooner who had joined One-Arm Ginger in the attack on Captain Gallows and been drowned. Now there he was, not drowned at all, but alive and breathing and smiling. Ozzie Twitch!

"We figured you couldn't swim!" I blurted out.

"Not a stroke!" replied the harpooner. "But a sea lion gave me a poke in the air, thankee. And I caught hold of the anchor chain and pulled meself up. Been hiding aboard ever since. Your one-armed shipmate swore there's tons of pirate treasure aboard. Be a good cabin boy and lead me to one of them green ship's eyes, and I'll be gone and happy. Where'd the captain hide the plunder?"

I was made quickly aware of the emeralds in the hem of my coat and almost gave them a reassuring tap. "If I knew, I wouldn't tell you, sir!"

"No? In that event, I'll be obliged to wring your cabin boy's neck."

"You'll have to wring mine first," bellowed

Captain Fitch, who had come up from the shadows behind me.

At that, the harpooner leaped out of the bunk and bolted into the fo'c'sle darkness and was gone.

"What was that all about, lad?" asked Captain Fitch.

"He was a stowaway."

"A bad lot, stowaways."

"Yes, sir."

Said the captain, "I was bound to follow you."

"Me?"

"I heard you speak English."

I stood astonished. "Not me, sir!"

"No Mexican would yell 'ouch.' He would say '*ay!*'"

"I scraped my hand on a turnbuckle."

"You must be an American."

I fell silent.

"Don't worry," said the captain. "I not going to turn you over to the Mexicans. They can't be bothered with an American cabin boy. Don't you know there are several of us Americans living here?"

"No, sir."

"We became citizens of Mexico and took Mexican wives. We are Californios, like our neighbors. So far the war has not touched us. Where are you from? Homesick?"

"Boston. Yes, I think so."

"Where is this ship bound for?"

"Nowhere," I said. "The captain has dropped the anchor here for good."

"Then how do you plan to get home?"

"I don't know, sir."

"That will call for patience, lad. There is no shortage of American ships out of sight in the Pacific. One year, the custom people logged in over six hundred traders and whalers! Imagine! Some ship's captain who hasn't heard we're in a war is bound to turn up for water and provisions. Watch for the stars and stripes! That'll be your voyage home!"

I burst into a smile. The stars and stripes! Yes, I'd keep my eyes peeled for flags.

Captain Fitch started back up the ladder but stopped for a backward glance. "If our eager militia gives you any trouble, lad, they mean well. Avoid the justice of the peace, who must go by the book. Send for a tavern keeper, Sam'l Spoons."

"Him?"

"You've met the devil?"

"I have, sir."

"Oh, he's on both sides of the law and never troubles himself with honor. But he can fix anything."

"I hope I will not have to trouble him," I declared.

"Good luck," said Captain Fitch in his rough voice, but with a broad and honest smile. I felt reassured to know a friendly face in this foreign town.

CHAPTER ○ 10

A search of the ship was made, but the harpooner had vanished like a ghost. Calcutta thought he might have slipped in among the townspeople when they returned ashore in their crowded boats. Captain Gallows didn't seem concerned, hardly giving the matter a shrug. He turned in early, obviously pleased with his great success as a host.

Morning arose in an orange fog of sunlight. Captain Gallows slept late. When he finally roused himself, we went ashore, saddled the rented horses, and started back up the coast.

The fog burned off, and the day now looked freshly washed and scrubbed.

My eyes kept scanning the flashing blue ocean to my left. There was no ship out there flying the American flag. There was no ship out there at all.

When we reached Rancho Candalaria, I saw the dead estate rising from its own ashes. Pigs were rooting in the pens. Black cattle had been turned loose to graze on the hills. Juan Largo had hired Indian vaqueros to round up wild horses and break them to the saddle. Gardeners were tending the neglected grapevines. Women sat in the shade of a peppertree and ground dried corn in three-legged granite mortars for tortillas. The kitchen chimney was cleaned and fresh fires started in the ovens. Cooks brought forth pots of pozole, a thick hominy soup smelling of pork, for the quickly growing population. I watched it all.

Captain Gallows was clearly impressed to see his mustached *mayordomo* quietly issuing orders in two languages. Without a wasted moment, Juan Largo hired an Indian black-smith and a Mexican harness maker. He sent a cart to Los Angeles for glass to replace the stolen windows. As if decorating a festive cake, plasterers were already giving the house a fresh white icing.

"My compliments," said Captain Gallows.

"It is too early for compliments," said Juan Largo briskly. "And you are in my way. Manuel, we will start branding the cattle in the morning and shoeing the horses."

"But none of the rancheros brands cattle or shoes horses," said Manuel, pulling a sweat-stained rag down over his forehead.

"Then we will be the first," replied Juan Largo.

"My compliments, Juan Largo," the captain said again.

"I heard you the first time, Don Alejandro. And you are still in my way."

Captain Gallows burst out laughing and ambled off, clearly amused by the impudence of his stork-legged *mayordomo*.

Following along in Captain Gallows's dusty footsteps, I jingled the coins in my pocket. They weren't much, but I felt rich.

After the sale of the silks and spices and crockery aboard ship, the captain had ordered that the money be shared out. As cabin boy, I was entitled to a tiny share and now had a pocket jingling with heavy silver Mexican pesos. I had no idea what they were worth. I slept well, smiled a lot, and went days without thinking about home.

Outside the kitchen one morning, I caught sight of the frightened Indian girl cleaning a freshly caught barracuda. I watched her for a while, relieved that she was no longer scared out of her wits and screaming.

I approached. I didn't know her language and she wouldn't understand me, but I wanted to say something. I said, "What's your name?"

"Oliviana."

"You understand English!"

"Not often," she answered simply, and carried the fish into the kitchen.

I climbed a dusty peppertree and watched Juan Largo looking over wild horses in the corral. The ranch manager chose five to be broken for use around the ranch. I saw Captain Gallows return from the house, wearing an old Mexican straw hat he had found. He looked over the saddle horses in the stable. He picked out a stallion, tall and black, for a gallop around his rancho.

I was told to climb down from the tree and to pick out an animal. I pointed to a smaller horse, tan as dirt, with a luxurious mane. The Indian vaquero said the beast was recently wild, but was now broken and tame as a chicken.

I eased myself into the saddle. The animal

lost no time in reverting to his wild state. He leaped into the air. I could feel his back under me bending into a sudden horseshoe. I hung on. He snorted. He spun. I hung onto his mane. Then he gave a kick of his hind legs. That tossed me somersaulting through the dust.

"Shipwreck!" said the captain, grinning. "This is no time for play!" He made a chopping motion with his right hand. "Let's take these beasts for a ride. They need to know our voices!"

I didn't bother to dust myself off. I could feel the captain's impatient eyes on me. I hoped that Oliviana had remained in the kitchen and been unable to see me made a fool of by a dumb horse. She was almost as old as I was, and I bet she could ride any beast of a horse she wanted to.

I slipped my feet into the wooden stirrups. I had no choice but to try the horse again.

I shortened my grip on the reins and held them close and tight. I spoke firmly. Maybe he didn't understand English. He shook his head as if to jerk the reins out of my hand, but kept his legs still. I tried touching him with my heels. The horse ignored me. I tried again and made a sharp sound, like the cracking of a stick. That caught the attention of the horse. He took a gentle step forward. I was amazed. And then he took another step, as if he had only been trifling with me.

I didn't know whether to be pleased with myself or the horse. The captain rode out onto the rutted clay road. I followed.

We were quickly beyond sight of the ranch, picking our way through a fold in the hills. "Did you taste the hominy soup?" asked the captain.

"The pozole?"

"How do you know what it's called?"

"Is it a secret?"

"Ah, so you keep your ears open, Shipwreck. When I was a boy, in the old Spanish days, it was the smell of pozole that sometimes lured hungry Indians to the missions. The friars called it 'catching converts by the mouth.' But now all that is finished, *sí*? Now that Mexico is its own boss, it is the rancheros that catch them by the mouth. But at least we pay them, eh? Do you know what I am paying the Indian vaqueros?"

"Those horsemen?"

"Ah, the cleverest horsemen in the world! I will pay them a clever fifteen pesos a month."

I had counted my own pesos—I had twelve. Almost the equal of a vaquero! I could imagine the astonishment on my mother's face when I returned home and let the coins slide into her hand. Would she be impressed with me? The picture again rose in my mind of the festive orange parasol she had opened to see me off on the wild seas. Had her tears dried? Had there been any tears? I sometimes wondered if she had forgotten me before I was out of sight.

"Shipwreck!"

"Yes, sir."

"Stop dreaming. You will fall off that short-tempered horse."

"I'm awake."

"Were you dreaming of the young Indian girl? I saw you gazing at her. If you want to ask her name, I'll tell you how to say it in Spanish."

"I know her name."

"Indeed?"

"It's Oliviana," I said.

"Pretty name, eh?"

Then the captain made a sweep of his arm. "All this land is mine—I believe. Mine and the jackrabbits'!"

The birds stopped chirping. Rawhide lariats buzzed through the air and jerked the two of us out of our saddles. I felt myself flying in midair. "Hey!"

The horses, unburdened and so recently wild, ran free.

"Ah, señor! I have not had the honor of robbing you before! But I am new on these roads."

It was a woman's voice, as merry as a songbird's.

I found myself on my back. When I looked up, I saw a small woman in a feathered hat at the head of a ragged band of highwaymen. Their guns stuck out like the pins in a pincushion.

"Foreigners, it appears," she added in perfect English. "Such elegant boots!"

Captain Gallows brushed himself off and asked gallantly, "Shall we do you the courtesy of putting our hands in the air?"

"That formality won't be necessary," the woman replied. Her long hair hung over her shoulders in a glossy black fan. Mounted on a tall, rawboned horse, she was wearing velvet breeches, a green scarf around her waist, and a leather vest. "But you may throw down your gun, if you wish."

"My dear woman, I would like to accommodate you—"

"I am not your dear woman," she interrupted sharply.

"I intended only to give you the benefit of the doubt," the captain said. "It is impossible for me to throw down my gun."

"Don't be absurd, sir."

"Alas, I failed to arm myself for this hazardous journey. I shall not be so forgetful again, madam."

"Miss," she said, again correcting him. "But no one travels empty-handed. I'm sure you won't mind making a contribution to the poor."

"I shall be delighted. What poor are we talking about?"

She turned a little smile on us. I couldn't help noticing that when she smiled her face was pretty, but tired. "You can see that my men are in little more than rags. Look at my father, Hernando. The poor man doesn't even own a pair of shoes. My brother Pedro, with his elbows sticking out, is in need of pesos. So I must trouble you for your valuables!"

"A family affair, I see," said the captain. He lifted his straw hat and pulled off a leather money pouch hung around his neck. He weighed it in his hand. "I suppose you have a name, señorita."

"Have you foreigners not yet heard of Señorita Wildcat?"

"You are mistaken. I am not a foreigner." The captain cocked an eyebrow. "Señorita Wildcat? What an unseemly name to call yourself. It lacks elegance."

"It's what the rancheros have begun to call me. They are annoyed that we help ourselves to their cattle when we are driven by hunger. I was annoyed when a don himself grabbed me, and I scratched like a—"

"Wildcat. Have the rancheros no sense of chivalry?"

"None."

"I shall be honored to contribute to the poor of your choosing." Captain Gallows tossed his money pouch from hand to hand. "But does it require so many bandits to rob one man and a boy? I have seen smaller armies."

"Señor, help is cheap in California—even among bandits. Throw down your money."

Captain Gallows tossed the pouch to the

ground. If he were worried about the emeralds, his light and bantering manner revealed nothing.

A feeling came over me, like a sharp chill wind, that something was wrong. The emeralds. My right hand slid down to the hem of my jacket to reassure myself that the hard lumps were still there.

The emeralds were gone.

I had lost them!

My heart began to thunder. I looked at Captain Gallows. How could I tell him? I shrank back into myself, trying to become invisible. He'd hang me from the nearest tree.

Señorita Wildcat directed one of her men to pick up the pouch. "Now your jewelry."

"Señorita," the captain replied, confident and lighthearted. "As you can plainly see, I am not burdened with trinkets. Such trifles are not to the taste of a gentleman."

"Are you a gentleman?"

"A scoundrel by trade, a gentleman by instinct."

She gave her head a toss. "I have never met a gentleman who wasn't a scoundrel by instinct."

"Careful, Señorita Wildcat," the captain replied, with an air of mischief. "Wound the pride of a gentlemen and risk the consequences. The scoundrel may be obliged to challenge you to a duel."

She fired her pistol, almost winging his ear. "Because I am a woman, don't assume that I would decline. Was that close enough?"

I raised my eyes at the sound. Captain Gallows felt his ear to make sure it was still in place. "Quite close enough. I am charmed to have made your acquaintance, Señorita Wildcat." He made a chopping gesture with his hand. *"Buenos días."*

"Hold on, señor. Your red boots. They will fit my old father here with room to spare! Take them off."

From the captain's bantering manner, I was sure he thought his emeralds were safe in my coat. He sat on a fallen log and directed me to help pull off his boots.

I did what I was told, unable to look up. I couldn't swallow. My heart wouldn't stop pounding. Didn't he notice?

Old Hernando was overjoyed with this treasure. Señorita Wildcat looked at the captain in his stocking feet and smiled. "I'm sure you have many pairs of boots, señor. I will pray for you that we do not meet again."

"And I will light candles with the same happy thought, Señorita Wildcat."

She gave her men a shout. "*Vamanos!* Let's go!"

Off the bandits rattled through the willows and live oaks. As the gang disappeared, I caught sight of a slow smile bursting over Captain Gallows's face. "You see!" he exclaimed. "To a thief, a child has nothing in his pockets but marbles. As I suspected. You conducted yourself well. The emeralds are safe. Now then, I have not forgotten how to walk. *Vamanos!* Let's find our horses."

I stumbled after Captain Gallows. How
could I tell him what had happened—
that his emeralds were gone. Where could I
run off to? Hide with the jackrabbits somewhere? Forever?

How could I have lost the stones? When
the horse threw me? Along the trail?

I saw that it amused the captain to again feel the earth between his toes. He'd pulled off his stockings, remarking that he'd spent the first fourteen years of his life on bare feet.

We came upon our horses, grazing on grass and buttercups a quarter of a mile away. He seemed almost reluctant to settle himself back into the hard saddle. Mounted again, we continued into the foothills. I was silent as a mouse, but he was full of talk.

"It seems, Shipwreck, that California grows bandits as abundantly as it grows cows," the captain mused. "Did you notice what a ragtag lot they were? Stealing boots! Imagine! These juiceless outlaws have no pride in their profession! And a woman, at that. When I was a child, bandits rode about like hidalgos! Like royalty!"

I was barely able to keep my mind on what he was saying. We rode a little farther before a flash of deep contempt rose into his voice, and I looked over at him. "Hidalgos! That's what Don Simplicio fancied himself to be. How he strutted! How he swaggered, eh? Like a peacock! You look pale. Sick?"

"No, sir," I muttered. "You were talking about Don Simplicio."

"May the fleas of a thousand dogs infest his beard," said Captain Gallows, giving the horse a touch of his heels. "Pay attention, Shipwreck. It relieves me of the embarrassment of talking to myself, eh? So. When I was your age and living under Don Simplicio's whip, I heard a rumor that in all of Southern California, nine boys went to school. Imagine! I thought they must be very special. But what did they learn in school? I found out they learned to read. So I tried to teach myself. When Don Simplicio caught me attempting to read a book, he personally whipped me. I still have the marks on my back and a chip on my shoulder, eh? You see, he knew the value of ignorance in those like me who worked his land. He worshipped ignorance. That's what kept us chained to his rancho. An educated peon was like a sea worm in the timbers of a ship, eh? So I ran off, and now I am back and I intend to out-hidalgo the hidalgos!"

CHAPTER ✹ 12

CONTAINING AN EXCESS OF VILLAINS
AND A KICK IN THE DIRT

*L*ess than an hour later, the air filled with howls and wild shouts. I glanced around in amazement. Were we being held up a second time in a single morning?

"*Arriba las manos!* Up hands!"

Again horsemen flowed around us. Again I

saw a pincushion of weapons, but these were arrows cocked in bowstrings. And these were bare-chested outlaws wearing headbands and dusty rawhide leggings. Indians!

The captain ripped off his straw hat and threw it to the ground. "Mangy, no-account, noisy rascals! Go to splintered lightning! Blast the lot of you! Mexican outlaws held us up an hour ago! Look!"

He pulled out his pockets and let them hang like dogs' tongues.

"Have you pesky highwaymen no sense of restraint? The pack of you look hungry enough to eat bark off a tree. Is everyone in Mexico out of work and pouncing upon strangers? Haven't you heard? They are hiring at Rancho Candalaria. Now, out of my sight!"

The captain defiantly kicked his horse, and I was quick to follow. The band of outlaws stood frozen and bewildered by the captain's bristling contempt.

The excitement of it all made me forget the

emeralds. I was fearful of glancing behind as the captain advanced at an unhurried trot along the road. I hoped that the Indians were too numbed to follow. They had obviously never before met such a force of nature on two legs as this sea captain.

When I looked back, the Indians were fading away over the hills. The captain seemed afraid of no one. How had he grown up to be so fearless? I had watched the power of the captain's commanding presence freeze a flight of arrows. I wondered how I might grow up with that same bravado. I hadn't the courage to tell him what I had lost.

We turned back toward the rancho, riding in silence. Then he gave a sad shrug. "Unlucky devils," he said. "When I was a child, the Spanish missions made thousands of Indians work the orchards and herd the cattle for the hide trade. Shipwreck, I have seen mission lands the equal of small kingdoms! I remember when we pulled down the red-and-gold flag of Spain and raised the red, white, and green flag of Mexico. Did you see it on the flagpole in the plaza? Handsome, no? At last we had a country of our own. It was only fourteen years ago! Aye, and we took back the mission lands, except for a few acres. What could the padres do but turn the Indians loose, eh? What could the poor devils do but imitate what they saw so many Mexicans and foreigners do—steal cattle and take to the roads."

When we returned to Rancho Candalaria, I could hardly wait to dismount. I ran over to the corral where I had been thrown and started kicking through the dirt. I kicked and kicked. Finally Juan Largo noticed and came over.

"Lose something?"

"Anybody find anything?" I asked.

He shook his head and let me be. That's when I noticed Oliviana peering at me. Suddenly she rushed over and put a couple of rocks in my hand. The emeralds.

"When you were climbing in the peppertree," she said, "I saw the marbles fall from your pocket! Such big marbles!"

I was speechless. I smiled and managed to call up a little Spanish. "Thank you. A thousand *gracias*-es."

"*Por nada*," she answered, smiling back.

CHAPTER ● 13

"*Shipwreck!* Follow me!"

I was becoming accustomed to Captain Gallows's command. We were to return to town.

I had borrowed a needle and black thread from the seamstress and sewed the emeralds back in the coat with plenty of extra stitches.

It was becoming too warm to wear the coat all the time, but I was relieved to put it back on. I figured that I was hardly any different from a pouch of valuables the pirate might keep around his neck.

I'd be glad to reach San Diego again. Ever since Captain Fitch had mentioned that an American ship might come blundering into the harbor, I had felt a renewed hope of finding myself a passage home. I'd keep my eyes peeled.

I didn't know exactly how I felt about the idea of leaving Rancho Candalaria and Captain Gallows. I found myself making machete chops with my hand, the way he did. And I even tried to imitate the captain's bold, fear-nothing walk.

When we reached San Diego, a few lean black cows were chewing weeds in the streets. Talk was in the air. Some fool was paying four dollars apiece for dried hides, and traders were arriving from the ranchos with hides by the wagonload.

"Where do you intend to store your goods?" asked the justice of the peace, lifting his hat and scratching through his black hair.

"I will rent a warehouse in La Playa," the captain said.

"You remember Sam'l Spoons at the Red Dolphin? He has a warehouse."

"I remember him," said Captain Gallows simply. "But, Judge, you must do something about the bandits on the roads. They are thick as fleas. Why don't your soldiers deal with them?"

I stood wondering how the captain, a bandit of the seas, could be feeling so righteous after being robbed by a bandit of the roads—and a tiny woman at that.

"Ah, the bandits," said Judge Bomba with a great, quivering sigh. "Our soldiers have hardly enough musket balls left to play a game of marbles—and not enough powder to fill a thimble. Months ago I petitioned General Castro to spare us a thousand musket balls and flints and powder. My pleadings have been ignored."

The bareheaded captain raised a hand to shade his eyes from the afternoon sun. "I will have shot and powder sent from my ship." And then he added with a shrug, "How do you expect to fight a war with the United States without ammunition?"

"We are hoping the Americans must have more important things to do than to invade us. Perhaps the army will be unable to find San Diego on the map."

"And if the American warships come by sea?"

The judge gave a hopeless shrug.

CHAPTER ● 14

*R*eturning to the ship, Captain Gallows gave a whistle through his fingers and called the crew together.

"Calcutta, see how much powder and shot we have left aboard. What we can spare, send over to the militia. The rest of you, arm yourselves! Guns, knives, and belaying pins. First thing in the morning we're going to set a civilized example, now that we're landlubbers."

"Speak for yourself," said Chop Chop, standing with his powerful sea legs apart, the better to support his bulk.

Said the captain, "I promised to turn you into gentlemen, but that will have to wait. We're obliged to scare the daylights out of the impertinent rascals infesting the San Diego roads. One of them nipped my red boots!"

Then he pointed toward the La Playa shore.

"Chop Chop, go fetch Sam'l Spoons. You'll find him in the Red Dolphin. Cabin boy, polish me up another pair of London boots. The black ones."

I found the boots in the captain's quarters. Outside, settling myself in the shade against the deckhouse, I set to work with brushes. But the afternoon shade kept drifting away as the ship swung on its anchor chain. I had moved to the starboard side of the cabin when Chop Chop climbed aboard with Sam'l Spoons.

The tavern owner gazed at me with a flicker of recognition. "Ain't you—?"

I said nothing, polishing away with the shoe brush.

"You are! Me hat's off to you, lad! Loyal to your captain, you was! Escaped me clutches slick as an eel dipped in lard!"

The captain, who'd been below with Calcutta to direct the gathering up of spare ammunition, appeared on deck and saw the tavernkeeper.

"Mr. Spoons, I'm surprised to find you still vertical, so to speak. Not dead yet? Hasn't anyone put a blade in your ribs in all these years?"

"Good day to you, Captain. Don't you see, I'm such a two-faced fellow that no one can creep up and surprise me."

"Come inside. Shipwreck, bring the boots and help me put them on."

Once inside the cabin, the captain seated himself in a Chinese red chair carved with dragons, and I began the labor of working on one of the long boots.

"Captain Gallows," the tavern owner was saying, "it gave me a fright, indeed it did, to listen while that officer of yours, Mr. Ginger, was plotting the other night to put out your lights and steal the coppers off your eyes."

"I'm sure you came heroically to my defense," said the captain with a scornful smile.

"Well, no. No, sir, can't say I did. Sam'l Spoons don't believe in putting his oar in other folks' business. But I reckoned that your one-armed, lowdown barnacle of a chief mate couldn't beat you in a fair fight. Or an unfair one. Even with all the help he brought along. I had the utmost confidence in you, sir."

The captain, growing impatient with the barkeep's flattery, gave his hand a chop and changed the subject. "I want to settle accounts."

Sam'l Spoons lowered his voice to a conspiratorial whisper. "You want to talk in front of your cabin boy?"

"Do you have anything to say you're ashamed of?"

"Not me! Not me, sir!" Then the tavern-keeper lowered his voice again and wiped his mouth on the back of his hand. He seemed to choose his words carefully, as if he were paying for them by the ounce. "Can I assume my messages found you, roundabout?"

Captain Gallows nodded. "Roundabout, aye."

"Nothing faster'n them China clipper ships."

"I presume this will settle accounts, eh?" The captain tossed a small pouch of coins into the tavern owner's lap.

"I won't bother to count it," said Sam'l Spoons. "You was born generous. Glad to be of service. Now ain't it a pity how Don Simplicio's hide ships get plundered? Spice Islands sea pirates, I hear."

"Pity."

"Is it true you're buying hides at four dollars each?"

"True."

"That's not going to go down easy with Don Simplicio. He's loading his last ship—the *Serrano* there, out the window. She holds forty thousand hides. But his cattle are stolen right and left—without any help from me, may I add—and I hear he needs another five thousand hides to fill the cargo hold."

"You hear a lot."

"Don't I!" The tavern owner laughed. "Well, I don't think Don Simplicio can pay your price. I heard he's already down to his last pesos."

"The skinflint was always down to his last pesos."

"Of course. You'd know better than I."

I finished with the captain's other boot and gave both of them final touches of the brush. It was clear as window glass that Sam'l Spoons had been spying for the captain and getting messages to him. *The Giant Rat of Sumatra* must have lain in wait in the Philippines for Don Simplicio's last hide ship to come lumbering along off Manila.

"Mr. Spoons," said the captain, "I will need to rent warehouse space. At your usual dishonest rates?"

"It will be a pleasure."

Captain Gallows rose, exercising his feet in his boots, and Sam'l Spoons humbly backed toward the door.

"Good day, Captain. Do you know the boy there put himself at risk to warn you of the mischief afoot? If I hadn't locked him up, One-Arm Ginger would have croaked the lad with his good hand, for sure. Still might."

"Sadly drowned, is Mr. Ginger," remarked Captain Gallows.

"You don't say? Why, he was in my tavern not an hour ago."

The captain lowered an eyebrow. I froze. The air stopped short in my lungs. That mangy Mr. Ginger still alive?

"If he wasn't alive," said Sam'l Spoons, "he was giving a fine imitation. And he carries a grudge. If I was you, lad, I wouldn't turn my back to the dark."

CHAPTER ○ 15

I was not the first to spy the squat,
three-masted whaling ship entering
the harbor. She was heavy in the water and
clearly homeward bound. An American flag,
bright as fireworks, was flying from her stern.

"Look at that empty-headed fool!" shouted

Sam'l Spoons, waiting for Chop Chop to appear and row him ashore. "Don't he know there's a war?"

My heart took a leap. There was my passage home!

I began stripping off my coat as I ran back to the master's cabin. But the captain was no longer inside. I threw the coat, with its heavy emeralds, across the lacquered Chinese chair. For an instant, I thought I heard a small snort from the captain's bunk.

"Who's there?" I called out.

Silence. I peered all around the cabin. I shrugged. There was no one there but me and my imagination.

When I returned on deck, Sam'l Spoons had found a speaking trumpet and was shouting at the whaler as she came alongside.

"Ahoy, you American blockhead! Where d'ya think you're going! You can't anchor here! Turn that windbag around! Don't you know you're at war with Mexico?"

I discovered Captain Gallows standing behind me.

"You planning to jump ship, cabin boy?"

"Look how heavy in the water she is!" I said. "She must be full and heading home!"

"The coat?"

"In your quarters."

"See, amigo?" said the captain. "I told you I could trust you. Shipwreck, I will be sorry to lose you."

"You won't need a cabin boy on your ranch. You'll have plenty of help."

"True. But who will look after you?"

"I can look after myself."

"Also true. You are learning the ship's ropes, but the world has other ropes. I was beginning to teach you, wasn't I? When you first came aboard, your chin was down to your stomach. Now you hold it up, like me, like a bowsprit, no?"

I took my eyes off the approaching whaler to face the captain. I think I must have puffed up my chest just a little. "Reckon so. Reckon I do."

"Who will I have to mutter to? Someone who has read a book or two, eh? A captain has his four ignorant walls for conversation. So I shall miss your company."

I was astonished. The captain would miss me? My own feelings rose and began to tumble about. Would I miss the captain's company? I would. But there before my eyes stood a homeward-bound ship. With a gulp in my throat, I gazed back up at the captain.

Sam'l Spoons, waving his arms, had caught the attention of the long-bearded captain of the whaler. "Head back to sea, you dunce! You'll be mousetrapped."

I saw the whaling captain begin to shout orders to his crew. Men were climbing up the ratlines. The helmsman spun the wheel into a blur. The ship came about sharply in the channel, a stone's throw off our port side.

"Have a safe trip home, Shipwreck," said Captain Gallows, grasping the speaking trumpet from the tavern owner, who took a moment to cross himself.

"Ahoy, Captain! Hold on. I have a passenger for you to take aboard!"

The captain of the whaler lifted a speaking trumpet of his own. "What's all this confounded shouting ashore? A war with Mexico? Great guns, sir! Have you lost your wits? Why aren't you shooting at us!"

"That can be arranged, Captain!" replied Captain Gallows. "Meanwhile, will you take an American passenger aboard? We'll send him alongside."

"Glad to oblige."

Captain Gallows turned to me, but I was already on the run. I was in and out of his cabin quicker'n scat. I reappeared slipping into the blue coat with the buttons down the front and the emeralds in the lining. I would stick to the captain awhile longer.

A smile, faint but firm, appeared in the captain's eyes when he saw me. He lifted the speaking trumpet to his lips again. "Belay that, sir! But do head out to sea. The militia boys ashore aren't practiced shots, so they just might hit you."

CHAPTER • 16

O" horses and saddles rented for a peso a day, half the crew of *The Giant Rat of Sumatra* followed Captain Gallows and me north. They remained more or less out of sight, lagging by a quarter of a mile.

"Shipmates!" Captain Gallows had instructed

them. "If bandits stop to make our acquaintance, I shall fire a shot. That will be your signal to rush forward and join the fight. We're obliged to make honest men of them!"

But it wasn't a man who confronted us on the beach road. Bursting out of a stand of wind-twisted pines came Señorita Wildcat.

"Arriba las manos!" she sang out, giving her loose black hair a toss. Several men behind her remained in the trees, their guns drawn. I could clearly see the bandit Hernando in his new maroon boots.

Captain Gallows held his fire. "Señorita Wildcat," he said. "I shall hate to make an unpleasant example of you. It doesn't seem chivalrous."

"Never mind chivalry or unpleasantness," she replied, straightening as she sat on her tall, rawboned horse. "Hands up."

"Seeking another pair of boots, are you?"

"This time, perhaps your stockings as well."

"And if I refuse?"

"As a matter of principle, I shall have to shoot you," she said.

"Is that ladylike, señorita? And what if I shoot you first?"

"A gentleman would not shoot first," she declared, smiling faintly.

"I do recall that you are a very good shot," said Captain Gallows. "I almost lost an ear the last time we met. But you are right. A gentleman, I suppose, would insist upon a duel."

"Do you think I would refuse because I am a woman?"

"I fear I am about to find out."

Her eyes flamed up. "I accept your challenge!" With a toss of her head, she slipped off her horse and planted her feet on the ground. She was touchy as gunpowder, I thought. And how tiny she was! "For honor or stakes, sir? What shall it be?"

"Why not both? If I fall, this young man will lead you to gems in my possession beyond your dreams. What have you to put up against such a treasure?"

I folded my arms as if to lock on the blue coat. What folly was the captain getting himself into?

She gave him a doubting look. "Let me see the jewels."

"You don't think I am stupid enough to carry them around like ship's cargo, señorita. On these roads? You have my word. What will you put up? Hernando's new London boots?"

"You may command my band of hungry outlaws!" she snapped. "Yours to feed and care for—if, after the duel, you are still standing! Most unlikely, sir!"

The captain turned to me. "Shipwreck, you witnessed the terms, did you not? If I am still standing, I win!"

I said nothing. The captain was regarding the duel as a lark. The bandit had already displayed her aim with a pistol. He'd seen how dangerous she was.

But almost as disturbing was the sudden thought that Captain Gallows might fire his pistol at a woman. No gentleman would consider such a bloody act! On the other hand, he wasn't really a gentleman. He was a pirate.

"Ready, sir?" Señorita Wildcat sang out, bristling with confidence. "Shall we begin?"

"A certain attention to details is called for. What weapons do you prefer?"

She shrugged. "Pistols will be fine."

Captain Gallows got off his horse. "Do you care to choose a dueling spot?"

"What's wrong with this?"

The captain kicked a toe into the land. "One could misstep in this beach sand. Will you allow me to select the place for our exchange of tempers?"

"Please yourself."

Captain Gallows looked into her eyes. "It is agreed, then? I have the privilege of choosing the spot?"

"Do you wish it in writing?" she asked scornfully.

"Your word will be good enough, señorita."

"Choose any silly place you wish."

"Splendid." Captain Gallows pointed his left arm straight out to sea. "We will hold our duel thirty paces due west!"

"Idiot," she muttered.

"That way!"

"You are pointing to the water."

"Indeed, I am. Thirty paces into the sea, Señorita Wildcat, and we may fire our volleys. Shall we begin?"

The surf was breaking noisily and trimming itself with white lace. I saw at once how the duel would end. The captain was tall. Señorita Wildcat was short.

"One!" called out Captain Gallows.

"Uno!" echoed Señorita Wildcat.

They began to march into the surf.

"Two!"

"Dos!"

"Three!"

Her voice had not lost its fire, even though she must have seen what might lay ahead. The bottom was falling away. The water would grow deeper. *"Tres!"*

"Four!

"*Cuatro!*"

When the waves began to break around her hips, Señorita Wildcat lifted her pistol high to keep it dry. The counting advanced as they ventured deeper into the ocean. Soon Señorita Wildcat was up to her elbows in water, but she refused to quit.

"Fifteen!"

"*Quince!*"

"Sixteen!"

When the captain reached the count of twenty-five, the water was at Señorita Wildcat's chin. She held her head high, full of pride and fury and defiance. She marched boldly deeper through the surf.

At thirty, she was stubbornly underwater.

But her arm was held high, and she pulled the trigger. The pistol flashed in the general direction of the captain.

I tightened my eyes against the glare off the ocean. I barely saw the pistol fire. But I heard the bang of the shot.

The lead ball went wild. The captain was still standing, his head wet but above water. I didn't realize until that moment that I had held my breath. And when I let my air out, a ragged little laugh escaped with it. Protected underwater, the captain had seen that he'd be in no great danger from Señorita Wildcat below the surface. And if he chose to fire—

He raised the barrel to the blue heavens and pulled the trigger.

"I appeared to have missed you, señorita."

She wasn't listening. She was trying to swim back to shallow water.

The captain caught her by the waist and pushed her ahead of him through the surf. She fell onto the dry sand, catching her breath, and then turned her head to look at him.

"Scoundrel! If we duel again, we shall wait for the tide to go out!"

The tall Mexican said, "Notice that I am still standing. That was the sole condition agreed upon. You still have your honor,

Señorita Wildcat. But, alas, you have lost the wager."

Alerted by the gunshot, the ship's crew came galloping up. They began waving the ship's belaying pins like war clubs and firing their weapons. The outlaw band took one look and fled through the trees.

Captain Gallows held up a hand to stop the noise.

"Belay that, shipmates! Those highwaymen are now under my command!"

"They will not take orders from you!" exclaimed Señorita Wildcat defiantly.

"They will from you. Tell them they may work these roads, but only by holding up other bandits."

"That's nonsense," replied the young woman. She tipped her head to allow sea-water to run out of her ear.

"I can assure you, it is a profitable strategy."

"And if my men refuse?"

"*My* men, Señorita Wildcat. Mine. You're not going back on your word, are you?"

She flamed up. "I keep my promises!"

"So do I. Warn these rascals that if they defy these orders, my sea ruffians will hoist them from the yardarms of *The Giant Rat of Sumatra*. Seagulls will pluck out their eyes! As for you, Señorita Wildcat—"

But she was no longer listening. Striding to her rawboned horse, she threw herself into the saddle and started away. The bewildered band of outlaws rejoined her, but not before Hernando turned in his saddle.

"Señor, you want your boots back?"

"Keep them, with the compliments of Captain Gallows."

CHAPTER 17

CONTAINING A SPRINKLE OF RAIN
AND NEWS OF CANDALARIA

*F*or the first time, I saw Oliviana laugh. With dark clouds moving in from the ocean, an early summer shower fell over Rancho Candalaria like an unexpected visitor. Everyone ran for shelter, including me. I had been counting pigs in the willow-branch pens for Juan Largo.

Oliviana had been outside the kitchen, grinding corn for the noon tortillas, when the sudden gust of rain caught her. She sheltered the meal with her red apron, opened her mouth to the flinging drops, and laughed.

So I opened my mouth to the rain and laughed, too. "Tastes good, doesn't it?"

"Is clean," she replied, closing her eyes against the raindrops.

"Did you hear the mountain lion last night? Juan Largo said he found tracks this morning."

"My uncle was killed by a mountain lion," she said.

"I'll be thundered."

"Now I have left only my aunt, Mariana. There in the kitchen. I used to have a dog, Pablo."

"What happened to him?"

"Gone." She gave a shrug. "Gone."

Her aunt leaned out of the kitchen door and called to her in their own language.

Oliviana wiped the rain dripping off her nose, picked up the bowl of ground corn, and went inside.

Juan Largo came by on his stork's legs and paused. "How many pigs did you count?"

"I forgot to keep track. The rain."

"You call this rain? I've wrung more water out of my socks. Let's make sure we're not missing a hog. We can't have a cougar carrying off our livestock."

"I'll count again."

"Candle maker!" the *mayordomo* shouted to a gray-bearded Mexican crossing to a work shed. "Felix! Don't make us candles like the ones Don Simplicio sells! *Comprende?* Full of air bubbles. And his candles are limp as slugs! Light a match to the wick and they bend over. Give our candles some pride, *sí*? Some backbone?"

"If you will render me some hard fat to add to the tallow, my candles will stand like cathedrals!"

"You shall have it!"

Before my eyes, I was seeing Rancho Candalaria transformed into a small village able to take care of itself. Indian women were making hard soap for the rancho and more for Don Alejandro to sell. A harness maker had set to work. Mexican brick makers were molding adobe bricks, and masons were repairing the walls of old rooms. I supposed that Captain Gallows meant to have a rancho as bold and self-sufficient as the ones he had envied in his childhood.

Juan Largo kept hiring new help, and I was certain that I recognized a couple of bandits among them—Indians in worn rawhide leggings, who had been scared off weeks before by Captain Gallows's blustering manner. They were put to work below the cliffs to catch fresh fish for the ranch.

Captain Gallows now wore his Mexican clothes every day and was pleased when anyone addressed him as Don Alejandro. When he rode off without me, as he did to examine the records in the old Spanish mission, he warned me not to stray off the ranch. "No harm can come to you here. Jimmy Pukapuka will keep an eye on you, *sí*?"

Don Alejandro returned from the mission bursting with happiness. "She kept her promise!" he shouted on the veranda, needing to tell anyone and everyone.

"Who?" I asked. I could easily guess. Candalaria?

"Candalaria! She did not marry! I asked the priests to search again. Nor did they bury one, except a white-haired Candalaria with a limp! We looked through the mission records. Nothing! Old Padre Jaime recalled that my Candalaria ran away from Don Simplicio and vanished like a puff of wind years ago."

"Your sister, sir?" I stopped to realize that I had no idea who Candalaria really was. "Your wife?"

"Wife? She was eleven years old! We were orphans together in Mexico City. We were transported here together into the hands of Don

Simplicio. When I ran away, I swore to her I would be back for her and make her a queen. And here I am!"

He lowered his voice and bent closer. "Don't lose the emeralds, eh? They are for her!"

CHAPTER 18

ENTER THE MAN WITH FLEAS IN HIS BEARD

*T*he road was still damp from the summer shower when a carriage drawn by four matched horses pulled into the courtyard of the Rancho Candalaria. Chickens flew out of the way as if shot from a cannon. The harness maker paused to admire the carriage's oiled leather trappings. Oliviana's aunt, in the kitchen doorway, crossed herself and shut the door.

I had picked up a deep sliver, cactus needle, in my left hand that Captain Gallows insisted on prying out himself. Through the window I watched the carriage arrive. A moment later, Calcutta, who had taken a fancy to a Mexican hat with a brim as wide as his shoulders, came into the main room. "Some old man wants to see you," he announced.

"Then don't keep him waiting," said the captain.

"He's carrying a walking stick big enough to brain you with."

"He looks angry enough to use it, does he?"

"Aye. Steam coming out of his nose, like a bull."

"I've been expecting him."

Moments later a man with coarse white hair walked briskly into the room and pointed his walking stick at Captain Gallows. "Are you the imbecile paying four dollars for cowhides?"

"I am."

"I am Don Simplicio."

"I know who you are."

Don Simplicio lowered his cane. "Then you know the business of my ranch! Hides!"

"El Rancho Buena Vista? So much land the coyotes get lost in it. *Sí*, I know it well. Hides. Is something troubling you, Don Simplicio? One would think you had fleas in your beard."

"If you were on my land, and I were not a civilized man, I would have you horsewhipped."

"Oh, you did, señor, many times."

The old man narrowed his eyes and looked down his leathery, suntanned nose. "Who are you?"

"A cattle rancher and dealer in hides and tallow and candles and soap. Like you, Don Simplicio."

The eyes of the old man were smoldering. "See here, young man, I was dealing in hides before you were born. I have a ship half loaded for China. My cattle are gone. But no one will sell me hides to fill my ship's holds. They are selling to you. You must quit this nonsense. You will ruin us both, señor!"

"I think not."

"I assure you! If I have to meet your price, you will ruin me."

"You have ruined others." Captain Gallows didn't bother to look up from his project of endlessly extracting the cactus needle from my thumb.

"What? Who are you, señor?"

"Orphans grow up, Don Simplicio."

"Eh?"

"Don't you remember a boy fresh from Mexico City? A boy named Alejandro?"

"I do not."

"How quickly we forget those we mistreat, true? But you mistreated so many of us. I have come to settle the score."

Don Simplicio stiffened. He froze. His eyes dulled. He appeared as if his mind had gone spinning backward through the years. And then, without another word, he turned on his polished heels and left the room.

Don Alejandro pulled out the cactus needle.

I said, "Ouch!"

*J*immy Pukapuka raced to Rancho Candalaria with the news that an American warship had been sighted off the headland.

"Her bottom is stuck in the shoals! She's waiting for the tide to rise! The war is in our lap! And some Mexican general has come aboard *The Giant Rat*, and he's giving orders, but none of us understands him!"

Captain Gallows's eyes shot around for a saddled horse. Juan Largo, mounted on a gray stallion, was almost at the gate. The captain whistled him back and replaced him in the saddle. He shoved his boots into the blocky wood stirrups. "Is there time to take *The Giant Rat* out to sea? To safety?"

"No. Yes. Maybe," replied Jimmy Pukapuka.

Without another word, Captain Gallows kicked and raced the stallion out of the courtyard.

I watched him disappear into the trees, dirt flying from the horse's hooves. I was left behind. Had Captain Gallows forgotten that I was standing there? That I existed? If *The Giant Rat of Sumatra* was setting out to sea, shouldn't I be along?

Picking out a fresh mount and transferring the sweat-stained saddle, Jimmy Pukapuka went flying after the captain.

I was surprised at my own feeling of abandonment. The captain might have spared me a glance. A quick word. Had he expected me to remain on the ranch?

I shrugged with uncertainty. I'd become accustomed to following along where the captain went. What if the tall Mexican and *The Giant Rat of Sumatra* didn't return? What was I supposed to do with the confounded emeralds in my coat?

For the first time in a week, I thought about home. Where did I belong? On Rancho Candalaria? In Boston?

I discovered Oliviana staring at me as she carried a tub of water for the kitchen. I turned away and walked into the house.

I watched the ocean outside the windows, half expecting to see a fleet of American warships on the horizon. Later, when I discovered Captain Gallows's pistol lying on a chest, I ignored the thing. The captain had been in such a rush, he had forgotten to arm himself.

But then I was drawn back to the pistol. If the American warship was attacking, wouldn't the captain need his firearm? I picked it up. I wasn't sure what good a small pistol might be against a ship's cannons, but my decision was swift.

I stuck the pistol in the top of my trousers. It was a hot day to wear my coat buttoned, but I buttoned it over the pistol. I strode outside, making hand gestures to the Indian vaqueros to saddle my horse.

I looked back. Juan Largo was nowhere in sight. But Oliviana was still watching me. She seemed aware that I needed watching.

I gave her an innocent smile, and the moment the horse was saddled, I slipped my foot into the stirrup. I'd bring Captain Gallows his pistol, whether he needed it or not.

I allowed the horse to walk out the gate so as not to attract attention to myself. Once into the trees, I dug in my heels, and the horse began to rattle away.

CHAPTER ⚬ 20

I couldn't catch up. The captain and
Jimmy Pukapuka were nowhere in sight
over the brown hills and beyond the cliffs
toward San Diego. When my horse began to
blow, I took pity, slipped to the ground, and
walked the animal along the rutted road.

"But don't take your time catching your breath!" I told the beast. "I'm still in a hurry."

My mind kept leaping ahead. I just might present myself to the American sea captain and ask to be taken aboard the warship. The Americans would see I got home to Boston, wouldn't they? How much would Captain Gallows care that I was gone? In the way of seafaring men, he'd give a wave and a smile and forget me quickly, I thought.

I heard running water and found a small brook flowing out to the cliffs and down to the sea. I fell on my stomach and drank. The horse didn't have to be told.

"My eyes! If it ain't the ship's cabin boy himself!"

The familiar voice sent a shiver through me. I slowly turned my head. Against the blazing sun, I saw One-Arm Ginger and the harpooner standing over me.

"If you're looking for Captain Gallows, sir, you missed him," I said, hardly moving a muscle. "He must be clear to San Diego by now."

"Oh, we saw him plowin' by, all sails hoisted."

"It's not him we're looking for," added the harpooner.

"No, lad," said One-Arm Ginger. "The captain can go to blazes with me best compliments. It's you we're after, lad. You, cabin boy."

Sprawled and frozen, I slid them another look. I could hear the water rushing below my cheek. "You must be mistaken," I said, surprised at the steadiness of my own voice.

"No mistake about it!" replied One-Arm Ginger. "Mr. Ozzie Twitch here, he was hid about *The Giant Rat* where no one would think to look for him. Hid in the captain's own quarters, he was! Aye, and he saw you rip off your coat, did he not? You felt the lumpy lining with your fingers, did you not? And then you fled back on deck."

"I did and he did," said the harpooner proudly. "And out I pops to have a look, and what do you suppose I find? Now, who would sew common rocks in his coat, I ask ye?"

Said the one-armed man, "Mr. Twitch had the wit to pull apart the stitches enough to see a flash of green. He was about to make off with your coat—"

"But in again you pops and grabs the infernal coat and off you rushes back out."

I clearly remembered the moment when an American whaler had come blundering into port. I'd changed my mind about deserting Captain Gallows and leaving the coat behind.

One-Arm Ginger ran a scuffed finger under his nose. "Now, the moment Mr. Twitch told me about that sparkle of green, I calculated what it signaled. Emeralds is green, ain't they, lad? And just what green emeralds might they be, eh, cabin boy? Why, the eyes of the blinded *Giant Rat of Sumatra* herself! Am I correct? And now we overhauled ye at last, wearing the very coat buttoned to your neck!"

I could feel the pistol concealed against my

stomach. I remained flat to the ground, wondering what Captain Gallows would expect me to do. But the moment I felt One-Arm Ginger's fingers grasp at the coat, I spun over. Rolling to my back, I drew the pistol from my waist and held it firmly with both hands.

"Back off, sir!"

One-Arm Ginger sprang back with astonishment. And then his red-nosed face cracked a smile. "Lawful mercy, lad! That was cleverly done! Slick as butter! Why, I do believe you'd explode that trifle and send yur old friend to red-hot perdition!"

"You're no friend of mine. And you'd best back off."

"Certainly, lad. Come, long, Twitch. The boy's hoisted a battle flag, and I say we salute it."

He gave a small, clumsy salute and turned his back to me. For a moment my muscles eased up. But the next moment, One-Arm Ginger gave a sharp backward kick with the heel of his boot. Loose dirt flew and struck my face.

I sprang up, half blinded. But Twitch was already charging into me. I felt One-Arm Ginger's powerful fingers closing around my small fist and the pistol. I held on with all my strength, and the gun fired.

For an instant, I think his muscles froze as well as mine. When it became clear that the shot had gone wild and that neither of us was shot, One-Arm Ginger chuckled with a burst of scorn. "My patience, lad! Don't you know I catch pistol balls between me teeth and spit 'em out?"

I bit the man's thumb even as the harpooner caught my legs and brought me to earth. The pistol went flying like a pulled tooth and gave a twist in the air. It tumbled down the cliff, kicking up puffs of dust.

My heart sank.

One-Arm Ginger gave his thumb a hard shake. "Now, that wasn't a polite thing to do, lad. Me patience's at an end! Let's have that infernal coat!"

Mr. Twitch began pulling at the coat sleeve

while One-Arm Ginger caught the collar. I reckoned that I was beaten, but a fury rose in me and I stubbornly folded my arms to lock the coat to my chest. Isn't that what Captain Gallows himself would have done?

The men tugged on the coat, then stopped short.

"Arriba las manos!" came a shout in the air. "Hands up!"

I gazed up at men on horseback surrounding us, their guns drawn and teeth bared like the dreadful jaws on the figurehead of *The Giant Rat of Sumatra.* My heart gave an awful leap and began to thunder. And then I recognized the voice of their leader. I took a breath, hugely relieved to see Señorita Wildcat on her tall, rawboned horse.

CHAPTER 21

"*Is* that how you foreigners rob travelers?" exclaimed Señorita Wildcat. "And a mere boy at that! You give dishonesty a bad name."

"Señorita," said One-Arm Ginger, attempting to brush himself off. "Miss, if you plan to empty our pockets, you'll find nothing but dust and a live flea or two. So we'll lift anchor, if you don't mind."

She made a short chop with her hand as she turned to her men. "Wrap them up like sausages," she said. "We'll deliver them to the jail. I keep my promises, even the foolish ones."

I stood transfixed. Had she seen Captain Gallows give his hand a chop the way she had just done?

Rawhide ropes were thrown out even as the harpooner attempted to run. I slipped down the shallow cliff and found the pistol. After scrambling back up, I hesitated while the two men were being disarmed.

"Ramón, my father," she called out. "See that they are wrapped tight. Help him, Luis, my brother."

My eyes fixed on Señorita Wildcat. Her father, Ramón? When she'd taken Captain Gallows's boots, hadn't she called her father Hernando? How many old fathers did she have?

"Thank you, miss," I said.

"You speak like an American," she replied, flashing me a smile.

"I am."

"We are at war. Then perhaps I should deliver you to jail as well."

"I'd be obliged if you don't. That thing you did with your hand, do Mexicans do that?"

"What thing?"

I sliced my hand through the air. "Like that."

"Like a machete, you mean? Do I still do that?" She gave a little laugh. "Yes, something I must have learned as a child."

"The captain does the same thing."

"Who?"

"The man you fought the duel with. Captain Gallows."

"Well, you may tell your Captain Gallows that I have caught him a pair of bandits. That was our bargain."

I found myself studying her like a puzzle. She had one too many fathers. "Maybe you'll want to tell him yourself," I said. "Did you notice that ship in the bay, miss? The ship with the figurehead of a rat? If he's not there, I guess he'll turn up at the ranch."

"He has a ranch?"

"Rancho Candalaria."

She paused. "What a curious name."

"Is it?"

"But common," she added.

After tying One-Arm Ginger and the harpooner to their saddles, the men remounted. Señorita Wildcat gave the merest nod of her head, and the horsemen spurred their horses. She lingered a moment and then started after them.

Words rose to my throat without any help from me. Astonishment rose with them. Where had such a windblown thought come from?

"Good-bye, Candalaria," I called out.

That would stop her in her tracks, wouldn't it? Unless she wasn't Candalaria and rode on.

She rode on. I felt crushed. I had made a

wrong and stupid guess. She wasn't an orphan. She was just Señorita Wildcat, fathers and all.

But then she hauled up on the reins, as if unable to resist a second thought. Her horse reared on its hind legs and spun around. She gazed at me. I hoped she would advance toward me. And she'd say, "How do you know my name?"

But she just peered at me. And then she turned the horse back around and rode off after her men.

CHAPTER ⊙ 22

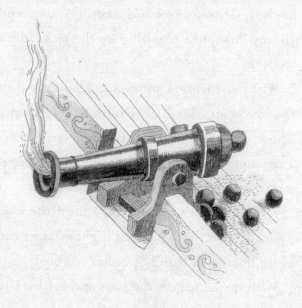

I saw the warship for myself. She had the
sails raised on all three masts as she
tried to blow herself off the shallows. Her
row of square gun ports were open on her lee
side, and the mouths of brass cannons
gleamed in the midafternoon sun.

Closer in, *The Giant Rat of Sumatra* still lay at anchor. I could see Captain Gallows and Jimmy Pukapuka climbing up the jack ladder to deck.

Without losing a moment, I pounded on the door of the Red Dolphin, but Sam'l Spoons had locked it and fled the war. Others I saw standing on the roofs of the hide houses, peering at the warship stuck in the mud.

I ran around to the back, found the oars where I'd left them my first night ashore, and again borrowed Sam'l Spoons's rowboat.

With my hands on the oars and my back to the ship, I had a clear view of the small Mexican militia advancing along the bay road.

I was soon at the side of *The Giant Rat,* even as the crew began to rotate the squealing capstan and raise the anchor. I tied off the boat to steady it in the swells of the incoming tide so that I could catch the jack ladder. Up I went and on deck. Not ten feet away stood Captain Gallows, still in his Mexican trousers with the silver buttons down the sides.

He was shouting orders, while at the same time angrily addressing a Mexican officer with sleepy eyes and thick sideburns that swept under his nose like fishtails.

"Amigos! Raise all the canvas you can! General Castro, I have no interest in helping you escape. Sahibs! Man the guns! General, I am putting you off! Shipwreck, what are you doing here? Take the general ashore."

The officer was sputtering with anger. His gold collar had popped open. "But the Americans are looking for the commanding general. If they find me, I will have to surrender."

"Without a fight?" snapped Captain Gallows.

"The cannons in the fort were spiked years ago! Fight with what? Look at the warship out there! The *Cyana* herself! Count those twenty-two guns!"

"I have," replied Captain Gallows.

"Clear the bay while you can, or she will blow you apart!"

"But what a disgrace for Mexico that

nobody fights for her. Ah, cabin boy, is that my pistol? *Gracias.* Now, if you will be so kind as to take General José Castro ashore."

My eyes must have flared. "But I want to stay aboard!"

"This is not your fight. Quickly, now!"

"No, sir," I said.

"What's this? Mutiny from a cabin boy? I shall have to hang you, eh?"

"Sir—"

The captain turned his back to me and lent a hand at the capstan. The general tightened his collar angrily and led the way down the jack ladder to the rowboat. I followed.

We reached the beach as the militia came marching in. The general immediately took command and turned them around to escort him back to town.

I climbed to the roof of the Red Dolphin for a better view of the warship. I saw the sails rising on *The Giant Rat,* but the ship remained tethered. The anchor chain looked stiff as a pole.

I could make out Captain Gallows and Jimmy Pukapuka and Calcutta struggling at the long handles of the capstan. Then it dawned on me. The anchor was fouled. Caught below. *The Giant Rat of Sumatra* could go nowhere.

It gave me a sense of relief. Captain Gallows wouldn't be so headstrong as to engage in a fight at such a disadvantage.

As I watched him shouting orders, it struck me that we now were obliged to regard ourselves as enemies.

I belonged to the other side. To the Americans. I no longer had any business aboard *The Giant Rat of Sumatra,* attempting to fight for the honor of Mexico.

The U.S.S. *Cyana* finally cleared the shoals. She turned and came cruising down the channel, taking in sails.

The Giant Rat of Sumatra fired off two of her deck cannons in blossoms of white smoke. For a moment the Americans might have taken it for a two-gun salute. I saw the cannonballs fall short, creating great splashes.

The warship fired back, taking down the sea rover's tall mainmast.

The sight of it falling stopped my breath. Captain Gallows was as often in the riggings as elsewhere aboard the ship. He might have been hit.

No. There he was, like a jack-in-the-box, making a chop with his hand. *The Giant Rat* lit off another cannon. The ball came hurling high in the air. In an instant, the warship let fly another volley. The pirate ship lost another mast. She sat wounded and disabled, but afloat.

I saw Captain Gallows rise again from a great spiderweb of shrouds and ropes and fallen ratlines. He straightened and gave the American captain a salute and a smile. I took it to be one of admiration for the artistry of its gunners. But it was just as clear to me that the smile was for himself. No one could say that Mexico had given up without a gallant broad-side. He fired off a final volley of cannonballs.

The warship found an anchorage and lowered a launch. A marine guard, some still visibly seasick from the voyage, steered for San Diego itself. I lost sight of them, but under the blue sky I could make out the tall flagpole in the plaza across the bay.

I saw the Mexican flag come down. San Diego had been captured. I watched the American flag rise and billow out like a sail in the late afternoon sea breeze. I felt immediately closer to home.

But how could I regard Captain Gallows as anything but a friend?

CHAPTER ○ 23

*C*aptain Gallows came ashore with several of his crew. None of them bore more than a battle smudge of gunpowder here and there or a new rip in his clothing. They looked up curiously at the American flag snapping above the windy plaza. The entire village seemed to have come outdoors, even the few Americans, with all eyes gazing at the foreign flag. Everyone seemed to be talking at once and muttering the same thought. So! Is the battle finished? Does San Diego no longer belong to Mexico?

"Captain Gallows," said Judge Bomba, carrying his white linen coat hooked from a finger over his shoulder. "I am afraid you must regard yourself as under arrest."

"On what charge?" replied the captain, lengthening the stirrups on his horse.

"A young woman covered in church veils has delivered into our hands two road bandits as tightly bound as mummies. The one-armed ruffian declares that you are a notorious pirate. A buccaneer, amigo! And you our sudden hero! We saw you thumb your nose at the American warship. Of course, the charge against you is nonsense, but the villain is prepared to swear to his charge."

"But it's true," said Captain Gallows with a simple shrug. "I have a modest fame as a rogue and a villain in waters across the world."

The justice scraped his jaw thoughtfully with the back of his hand. "It saddens me to hear that. But we don't have room in our little jail for three."

"I give you *The Giant Rat of Sumatra.* Her sailing days are finished. She will make you a fine jail."

"And a splendid fine can be charged against you, paid in full," replied the judge, a smile rising like dawn on his face. "But it occurs to me that I cannot arrest you for piracy in oceans across the world. Those longitudes are beyond my jurisdiction! I am afraid you will be obliged to be judge and jury in your case and punish yourself."

"I shall be merciless," said Captain Gallows, only half jokingly, it seemed to me.

"I would give some legal weight to those broadsides you fired at the Americans! You appear to have survived the battle without a scratch!"

It was a wonder, I thought. And since *The Giant Rat of Sumatra* was in ruins, and now given away, I reckoned that Captain Gallows's pirate days had ended.

It was only then that big Captain Henry Fitch joined everyone at the flagpole, carrying a puppy in his arm.

"No one seems too upset to be under the American flag, have you noticed?" he said.

"I think some would have preferred the British," remarked the justice.

"Almost anyone would do, yes," remarked the big trader. "Our government in Mexico City neglected us like an unwanted child. They viewed California as fit only for Indians, jackrabbits, and missionaries! And speaking of the unwanted, this pup is the last of the litter. I promised my wife I'd find a home for the rascal." He turned to the justice. "How about you, Judge Bomba?"

When the justice shook his head, I spoke up. "I'll take him, sir."

"Done!" said the trader, handing over the dog before I could change my mind. "His name is Señor Behind-the-Oven, which is where he was born, but call him what you wish."

"Yes, sir," I said.

Without a pause, Captain Fitch turned to the judge. "Your honor, I promised Don Simplicio I would fetch you. He's dying, you know."

Even as I snugged the pup at my elbow, I saw Captain Gallows's head snap around. "What's that?"

"Dying," repeated Captain Fitch. "As justice of the peace, Bomba, you're the only one he trusts to notarize his will. Not that he has anything left in his estate."

"You must be mistaken," said Captain Gallows crisply.

"I assure you, I am not. When his wife died, his heavy sorrows turned the old scoundrel inside out. How could he join her in heaven, you see? He tracked down those he had mistreated and provided them with land and cattle of their own—those he could find."

"He never tracked me down!" Captain Gallows exploded.

"Who could? And secretly he has been building orphanages where they are needed most, from San Blas to Monterrey to Mexico City. Never did he permit his name to be used. It was his punishment. And who would have believed the old miser had a beating heart? He even borrowed funds from me to keep building. Now his last peso is gone. He ruined himself."

I saw the color drain from Captain Gallows's face. "No," he said icily. "I ruined him."

He turned away from the flagpole and I followed him, clutching the dog but thinking of the four-dollar hides. Mounting his horse, the captain called to the justice that he was no longer buying hides at any price.

Several members of the crew of *The Giant Rat of Sumatra* decided to remain in San Diego until they could find another ship to their taste. Calcutta and Trot and Jimmy Pukapuka joined Captain Gallows on the march back to the rancho. Three pack mules bore their many sea chests.

I carried the puppy, fat as butter and only a little darker, clutched under my coat.

"Captain Gallows—" called out Jimmy Pukapuka.

"Don't call me that!" replied the captain in a cheerless voice. "Captain Gallows is no longer. I am Don Alejandro."

Don Alejandro sat gloomily and silently in his creaking saddle. Riding beside him, I gave him only one uneasy glance and quickly looked away. I sensed how tormented he was by what he'd just learned regarding Don Simplicio Emilio Charro. The captain had lavished years of hatred on a man who should have commanded his respect.

Wrapping his hands around the reins, Don Alejandro turned the horse around sharply and decisively and, without a word, began a flying gallop toward San Diego.

No words were necessary. I knew that he was racing back to stand before the dying ranchero and make his solemn apologies.

CHAPTER ⚬ 24

I was eager to reach the ranch at last and to pull the surprise from under my coat. "His name's Señor Behind-the-Oven, because that's where he was born, but you'll want to change it," I said, handing the golden puppy over to Oliviana.

"Mine? To keep?"

"Sure, to keep. Does he look anything like the dog you lost?"

"No, but I will love him anyway!"

She had come in from the old garden with a basket of carrots. The dog began mopping her face, and I said, "He likes you."

"*Si!* But don't you want to keep him for yourself?"

"I'll be leaving," I said.

Her expression darkened and she let out a small whimper. "*Aieee!*"

"I have a home. It's far away."

"Good-bye."

"I'm not going yet. I'll have to wait for an American ship. There should be lots, now that our flag is flying."

"Going to a home like this?" she asked, with a wave of her hand that seemed to embrace the entire ranch.

"Not like this."

She peered at me as if I must have lost my wits to turn my back on such a place.

"I have a mother in Boston. I want to see her again."

"A mother."

"I need to show her that I'm still alive. And then I'll see."

"See?"

"I want to know if she has an old orange parasol. Sometimes I wonder if it was someone near her, someone else I saw opening it up as my ship was leaving. We had already drifted quite a way from the wharf. Could have been someone else."

"I don't understand," said Oliviana, cuddling the dog and then holding him in the air. *"Gracias! Mil gracias!"*

"You're welcome. I may get back here someday, and that dog'll be grown! What are you going to call him?"

"I need to think."

"Plenty of time," I said, picking out a carrot and taking a bite. I started toward the door. Only then did I notice the tall, rawboned horse approaching.

Candalaria, wearing lace over her hair and shoulders, remained seated in the saddle. "You remember me?"

"You're Candalaria," I said.

"I think I am wasting my time. There are Candalarias all over Mexico!"

She seemed on the verge of turning the horse to gallop back the way she had come. What was she afraid of finding out? Quickly I held up the carrot to the horse. It turned its long face and picked up the carrot between its yellowing teeth.

"Don Alejandro just returned," I said. "Let me get him."

"Is that what he calls himself?"

"That's his name. Maybe you should come in."

"I choose to wait here."

I was sorry to leave her mounted, ready to flee at any moment. With fingers crossed, I hurried inside and found Don Alejandro standing at the windows, gazing at the sea.

"Candalaria is outside," I said in a bold voice.

Don Alejandro didn't bother to turn. "This is no moment for mischief."

"I'm sure it's her!"

"Don't be loco."

"It's Señorita Wildcat!"

The tall Mexican remained motionless. "Señorita Wildcat?"

"She looks ready to run. You'd better hurry outside, sir!"

"No need to hurry," said Candalaria.

I turned to see her standing inside the open doorway. Then she swept into the room like a typhoon wrapped in lace and winds of her own motion.

"Señor, why are you shouting my name about?" she asked. "What do you want?"

"Nothing, if your name is not Candalaria."

I saw her eyes flare with impatience. She stood, folding her arms and taking his measure from head to toe. "Who are you?"

"Do you remember a young Alejandro from Mexico City?"

"I don't recall."

"Let me look at you."

"Have you done anything but examine me since I stepped in?" she asked. "Like a jeweler through his eyepiece."

"I see no ring on your finger. You have never married? Shall I assume you have been waiting for someone?"

"You may assume what you wish!"

"You recall being an orphan, señorita?"

"I do not."

Don Alejandro took a step closer. "It's been years, but Candalaria could have grown up to look like Señorita Wildcat. Like you. There is a resemblance. I see it now."

"Look more closely and you will find no resemblance. I have never been in Mexico City. I am not an orphan. I have not been waiting for anyone. And lately I ply my trade along the roads. Keep looking for your Candalaria. It is not me!"

With a sharp and final chop of her hand, she turned and flew through the door. It shut after her as if slammed by a gust of wind.

I looked at Don Alejandro. Don Alejandro gazed after her. And then he began to chuckle softly.

"I am going to marry that woman."

"Señorita Wildcat?"

"Soon. As soon as possible!"

"I'm sorry I was wrong," I said. "I was sure she was the Candalaria you're looking for. Did you notice what she did with her hand? Just like you. And I figured she just called every old man, father.'"

"You were not mistaken. She is Candalaria. My Candalaria."

My spirits began to fill like a balloon. "You think so?"

"I could tell by the way her eyes examined me, still looking for the fourteen-year-old Alejandro who left, swearing to return for her. She waited all these years. And today she found him. Me."

I gave a small, hopeful nod. I crossed to one of the windows and caught sight of

Candalaria riding off under the peppertrees.

"I don't think she liked you, sir. She said she wasn't an orphan and that she'd never been in Mexico City."

"Think! I returned to discover her a petty criminal, stealing boots and trinkets. How humiliating, *no*? Candalaria will deny everything until I get her to the altar."

I was anxious to be convinced. But a sudden cloud blew across my mind. "Señorita Wildcat'll be caught. She'll have to go to jail!"

"True, and there's a most uncomfortable prison in San Blas, I'm told. But Señorita Wildcat broke Mexican laws. You saw what happened today. We are now under new laws! American laws!"

"But what if she breaks them!"

"We must stop her before she does anything so foolish." He threw open the door. "Calcutta! Jimmy Pukapuka! Hang it all, Juan Largo! Whistle up your vaqueros and bring that señorita back wrapped up in rawhide like a tortilla. Careful. She may bite!"

Then Don Alejandro turned back to me. "I must now trouble you for the eyes of *The Giant Rat of Sumatra*."

I was glad to be relieved of them at last. I ripped open the stitches at the bottom of my coat, and out tumbled the emeralds. It was almost August, and at last I didn't need to wear the warm, gosh-awful blue coat.

CHAPTER 25

*S*tanding on the adobe wall, I watched as
the United States troops, landed a
week before in San Diego, now marched past
Rancho Candalaria. They were on their way
north to plant the American flag in Los
Angeles.

I jumped down from the wall. Everywhere I looked, new things were happening around the hacienda. A blacksmith had set up his forge near the horse trough. A tailor had measured me for new clothes in the Mexican style, with silver buttons down the sides of the legs. Three seamstresses were at work making a wedding dress out of white China silk. Señorita Wildcat herself, in a room of her own, was making a summer hat she would wear after the wedding.

"I learned to make hats in New Orleans!" she burst out cheerfully at dinner one night. I listened quietly as her story quickly followed. Like Don Alejandro, she had run away from Don Simplicio. She had moved from mission to mission, finally running away from the Mission San Juan Bautista to the north. She had traveled to Texas and then New Orleans. There she had learned French, English, and how to make hats. Only weeks before, drawn to where she had grown up, she had returned with a trunkload of hats in the latest style to sell in San Diego.

But on the road, in a heavy rain, she had been stopped by highwaymen. Hoping to find something to eat, they had overturned the trunk in the mud.

"I had not imagined bandits could be so ragged and incompetent. But they were starving. They couldn't eat my hats, already ruined in the mud. Couldn't they see a feast of cattle grazing on the hills? Had they no imagination? Were they so afraid of the hidalgos? I decided with a snap of the fingers to make these poor fools equal to their profession. 'Follow me!' I commanded, and I learned to become a bandit. But truth to tell, the roads are empty, and a pair of maroon London boots was our greatest success!"

Day by day, war news drifted in. The white-bearded Mexican governor, Pio Pico, had fled, and all of California was falling to the Americans.

The morning arrived when I got dressed in my new clothes, pausing only a moment before a mirror to see if I recognized myself. Señorita Wildcat, in her wedding gown, stepped into the courtyard. Carriages were waiting to take everyone to the old mission in San Diego.

Hours later, shortly after noon, Señorita Wildcat stepped back into the bright sunlight under a new name. She was now Doña Candalaria. Large emeralds swung from her ears, as bright as green stars.

I heard a whisper. "Glass, of course." I lifted my eyebrows and smiled to myself.

The gems were so heavy on Doña Candalaria's ears that once the wedding party left the mission doors and reached the carriage, she fingered them as if she might pull them off.

"Doña Candalaria!" the judge exclaimed, after embracing the new bride. "You are free of the law! What can I charge you with? I am powerless! And what evidence do you offer? A pair of boots!"

"But handsome maroon boots. Made in

London. Surely a serious offense," said Don Alejandro.

"All right," exclaimed the judge with a patient smile. "We have a new jail. That ship in the bay with the lovely rat for a figurehead. Let yourselves in! Stay in jail as long as your conscience demands. Two weeks? A bit of hard labor clearing the debris? Yes, that will be your punishment. And then you may let yourselves out. And let that be a lesson to both of you!"

"I will learn my lesson well," said Doña Candalaria, at last pulling off the two large emeralds dangling from her ears.

Aboard *The Giant Rat of Sumatra,* the freshly married couple served out their sentences by clearing the war rubble from the decks. Doña Candlaria took her punishment seriously, scrubbing and polishing. Then it got into her head to climb below the bowsprit and give the giant rat a fresh coat of yellow paint. She wouldn't allow me to help her.

I remained aboard *The Giant Rat of Sumatra,*

waiting for an American trading ship to turn up.

Don Alejandro offered to pay my passage, but I refused. I needed to make my own way home. I needed to prove to the lingering voice of my stepfather that I could manage for myself. To my mother, too.

I was almost sorry to see the *Sea Horse* enter the bay under the Stars and Stripes and drop anchor. Her cargo deck was piled high and covered with canvas. A scruffy sea freighter, I saw, and I quickly found out that she was heading for New York and Boston with her hold packed with Chinese rugs and fire-works.

The master of the *Sea Horse,* a Captain Fred B. Kinne, said he might take me on as cabin boy. "Do you get seasick?"

"No, sir."

"You will, aboard the *Sea Horse*. She bucks and rolls something fierce."

"Yes, sir."

"She leaks. You won't mind bailing out?"

"No, sir."

"Food's terrible."

"I'm not hungry, sir."

Captain Kinne grinned. "You'll do. Sign here. The *Sea Horse* is speedy. Quicker'n lightning. Why, I'll have you home in five months!"

The time came for me to move my few things to a fo'c'sle bunk aboard the *Sea Horse*.

Don Alejandro forced a small money pouch on me. "For your education. I pass on the gift that was made to me when I was a cabin boy, *sí*? Remember the hen ship? Someday, Shipwreck, I expect you to command a ship of your own!"

I knew I must be blushing. A burst of pride made my face feel warm. I didn't want to disappoint the tall Mexican.

I wouldn't.

Doña Candalaria embraced me. "Come back to us."

My emotions were churning. I avoided the sight of the *Sea Horse* nearby in the bay. Why was I leaving the Rancho Candalaria?

I had to. Because I had to, I told myself.

The moment came to leave Don Alejandro and Doña Candalaria. I couldn't think of what I wanted to say—that I loved them as I wished I loved the woman under the orange parasol? But maybe that, too, would happen. I would find out. What I heard myself say was, "I wonder what Oliviana is going to name her dog?"

Then I turned and climbed aboard the *Sea Horse*. Lines were thrown off. Shouts and commands filled the air. Canvas rose to catch the wind. I took a last look at *The Giant Rat of Sumatra* and the tall Mexican and his wife I was leaving behind. I found my hand making a small, hesitant chop.

Then I heard a command. "Cabin boy!"

AUTHOR'S NOTE

*N*ovels are not plucked out of thin air. This one began with a question. What was wrong with the year 1846? Why were other writers ignoring it?

That was the year during the war with Mexico that a twenty-two-gun American warship sailed into the vast blue bay at San Diego. It captured the town, lowered the Mexican flag, raised the Stars and Stripes; and soon California found itself on the United States map. It was not an insignificant event.

But was it a good story idea? Depends.

Something was missing. Well, how about those rancho days, as they're called today, when California was a patchwork of Mexican cattle ranches the size of small kingdoms. In 1846 that feudal way of life was about to disappear.

That tempted me. I looked around for a place to open the curtains on the events of that momentous year. I might still be looking, except for a passing conversation.

I was having my eyes examined when Dr. Larry Garwood, one of the few doctors I know who reads novels, asked me if I knew about the giant rat of Sumatra. "Kind of," I answered. "Dimly. Refresh my memory."

Dr. Watson, who often boasted of the cases Sherlock Holmes had broken, mentions in "The Sussex Vampire" an affair involving the giant rat of Sumatra. What intrigues scholars is that Sir Arthur Conan Doyle never got around to scribbling a tale about that intriguing rodent.

I wasn't interested in writing a detective

story, but I was amused and captured by the exotic image. What might the giant rat have been? A carved and valuable temple statue? A pirate ship in the Far East, with a figure-head of a huge rat with jeweled eyes?

Yes!

I reached home with dilated eyes, turned on the computer, and began. I had in mind only the opening scene for a tale of the last days of Mexico in California. On a foggy night, an owl forebodingly rings the church bells. A pirate ship, baring the rodent's teeth of its carved figurehead, enters the San Diego bay in the fog and drops anchor at stage center.

Ten months later, I had the last scene. And the novel would complete a trilogy dealing with the chaotic years surrounding the California gold rush, begun with the sunny *By the Great Horn Spoon!*, continued by the darker *Bandit's Moon*, and completed now in the pages of *The Giant Rat of Sumatra*.

—Santa Monica, California

ALSO BY

Sid Fleischman...

The 13th Floor
Hc 0-688-14216-8

Bandit's Moon
Hc 0-688-15830-7

Bo & Mzzz Mad
Pb 0-06-440972-4

Disappearing Act
Hc 0-06-051962-2
Pb 0-06-051964-9

The Ghost on Saturday Night
Pb 0-688-14920-0

Jim Ugly
Hc 0-688-10886-5
Pb 0-06-052121-X

The Midnight Horse
Hc 0-688-09441-4
Pb 0-06-072216-9

Mr. Mysterious & Company
Pb 0-688-14922-7

The Whipping Boy
Hc 0-688-06216-4
Pb 0-06-052122-8

GREENWILLOW BOOKS
An Imprint of HarperCollins Publishers

www.harpercollinschildrens.com

Franklin Pierce University

00194606

DATE DUE

GAYLORD

PRINTED IN U.S.A.